MURDER ON THE BRAZOS

A Fen Maguire Mystery

Murder On The Brazos

Published by Jubilee Publishing, LLC
Paperback ISBN 9781958252079

Cover design: Streetlight Graphics
Editor: Teresa Lynn, Tranquility Press

MURDER ON THE BRAZOS

A Fen Maguire Mystery

BRUCE HAMMACK

Also By Bruce Hammack

The Fen Maguire Mystery Series

Murder On The Brazos
Murder On The Angelina
Murder On The Guadalupe
Murder On The Wichita

The Smiley and McBlythe Mystery Series

A blind former police detective with a special gift for solving homicides and a straight-to-the-point Boston debutante turned detective solve cases the old fashioned way... with brains and shoe leather.

Dive into the world of Smiley and McBlythe with *Jingle Bells, Rifle Shells.*

The Star of Justice Series

From chasing drug dealers to undercover operations to high-speed chases, campus assistant police chief CJ Harper and her state highway patrol husband, David, navigate a world of danger, deception, and intrigue.

Start your journey with David and CJ in *Long Road To Justice.*

See my latest catalog of books at brucehammack.com/books.

Chapter One

All was as it should be... until the body floated by.

A sigh escaped from Fen Maguire as he put his 4B sketching pencil away and mumbled, "At least this one isn't my responsibility."

The lifeless form eased to a stop in a tangle of flotsam, anchored by a fallen hackberry in the muddy water of the Brazos River. A third of the tree's roots clung to rusty earth, thirty yards from Fen's interrupted workplace.

Instead of punching 911, he called the non-emergency number to the Newman County Sheriff's Department and waited for a familiar voice to answer.

"Sheriff's department. How can I help ya'?"

The mental image of a woman with big hair and an encyclopedic knowledge of everything going on in the county flashed in front of him.

"Brenda, it's Fen. Grab a pen."

"Sheriff Maguire? Is that really you?"

Fen sighed. "Yeah, it's me. If you want to keep your job,

you'd best not let Sheriff Newman hear you call me sheriff. The last election took care of that title in front of my name."

"Ain't much chance of Miss Lori sticking her head in here on a Sunday morning, or any other morning, for that matter."

His gaze shifted back to the river; the body moved, turning face-up. Fen knew if he didn't get Brenda on task, she might talk for twenty minutes. "I'm on my property, about a mile down from the bridge. There's a body in the river, hung up on a fallen tree. Call Billy Ray. Tell him to get his team together and put in at the boat ramp by the bridge. There's a clear spot on the bank where I'm standing. The ambulance crew can help them get the body out of here."

"Do you want everyone to come to your place?"

"You know I don't want them here, but it seems I don't have a choice. I'll call Sam and have him open the front gate. He'll direct everyone to where I am."

"Any chance the victim's still alive?"

"No sign of life, and I don't swim in the Brazos. Call the justice of the peace on duty and tell him to come and make it official."

"Expect a crowd. You know how everyone loves to run lights and sirens."

The last comment didn't earn a response, so Fen pushed the red icon on his phone and shoved it back in his pocket. He spun around at the sound of a voice speaking over his shoulder, and instantly regretted the sudden movement as a bolt of pain shot from his right knee.

From the ground, Fen looked up, shook his head, and spoke through clenched teeth. "It's a good thing I don't carry a gun anymore."

Sam smiled and squatted beside him. "It's like the old days when we used to play cowboys and Indians. I'm getting you back for all those times you pretended to win and I let you."

Fen moved his bum leg, making sure it still worked. "How long have you been listening?"

"Long enough. I spotted the floating body downstream from the bridge and followed it to here while you were setting up your easel." Sam pointed. "It's bad karma that the body got hung up on that hackberry instead of floating downstream. It could have been someone else's problem."

"It's still not my problem, or yours. If anyone asks either of us, you were making your morning rounds, checking on cattle, and I found the body. That's all they need to know. There's no use in both of us having to write a report." Fen looked around. "Where's your horse?"

Sam stuck two fingers in his mouth and blew a piercing whistle. A saddled roan mare came running from behind a thicket of brush. Sam turned his attention back to Fen. "I'll open the gate for your visitors. Do you need your cane?"

"And an ice pack, if you have one in your saddlebag."

Sam went to Fen's four-wheeler and brought back a walking cane. "You need to get that knee fixed."

It was another statement that didn't earn a response.

Sam reached under Fen's arms and helped him to his feet. It took three steps for Sam to reach his horse and effortlessly pull himself into the saddle. The sound of hooves pounding earth gave way to a distant siren. The ranch foreman would make the first officers wait long enough to aggravate them. A small payback.

Fen hobbled to his four-wheeler and took the load off his leg by sitting in the passenger's seat. It wasn't long before a black-and-white Texas highway patrol SUV pulled alongside and the tall, lean figure of Sergeant Tom Stevens slid out, leaving his door open. He settled a buff Stetson on graying hair and spoke a single word greeting. "Sheriff."

"Not anymore," said Fen. "I'm glad you're the first on scene."

"Where's the body?"

Fen pointed. "Follow your nose. You can't miss him."

Sgt. Stevens moved to the river, pulled out his phone and took photos of the body and the bank leading down to the water's edge. He raised his voice enough to cover the distance to where Fen waited. "Did you get pictures of him before he got tangled?"

"Sort of. I took a short video. I also got still shots after the hackberry grabbed him. He was face-down until a little while ago."

"What about photos of the bank?"

"Yeah. No footprints prior to mine and yours."

A pickup truck from the sheriff's department dropped into the river valley, several hundred yards away. Emergency lights flashed and blinked, but the deputy had at least turned off the siren.

The highway patrolman climbed the incline, turned when he made it to Fen's side and looked at the river. "What do you think?"

"I'd start looking around the boat launch by the bridge." Fen dipped his head toward the body. "By the looks of him, he's been on the bottom for a while. It takes time for the gasses to form that brought him to the surface. I think he'd have hung up on something along the bank if he'd gone in farther upstream."

"Are you going to tell Sheriff Newman your theory?"

Fen held up his palms. "Leave me out of this. You know Lori and her father would like nothing more than to see me face-down in the river instead of whoever your victim is."

Tom placed a hand on Fen's shoulder and gave it a squeeze. "You honored Sally's wishes. I would have done the same thing."

A lump formed in Fen's throat, making it hard to swallow. Tom removed his hand and announced, "I need to make a few phone calls and get a state trooper to the boat ramp before Lori..." His voice trailed off. "You know what I mean."

"Do me a favor," said Fen. "Put out a call over your radio that you need the justice of the peace to respond. I don't want it known that I already told Brenda to call him."

Tom issued a quick nod. The door to his SUV closed with a thunk. Muffled, unintelligible words came from the highway patrolman's radio.

A pimply-faced young man exited the county patrol pickup. He was the last deputy Fen hired before his late wife's sister took the oath of office as the new sheriff.

Instead of speaking, Fen pointed to a spot on the river. The deputy nodded he understood, walked down the sloping river bank, put his hand over his nose and mouth, and returned to where Fen stood. "What should I do?"

"Remember your training. Take things one step at a time and do what your supervisor tells you."

"How do you secure a crime scene when it's in the middle of a river?"

Fen lifted his shoulders and let them drop. The answer to the deputy's question arrived as his radio came to life with the voice of Sheriff Lori Newman yapping like a Chihuahua. She demanded to know if any of her officers were on the scene yet.

The deputy swallowed, gave his call sign, and told her he and a state trooper were there.

"Tape off the crime scene."

"10-4. But, how? It's in deep water."

Silence.

Fen let out a groan. "Tell her to disregard your last transmission. You'll handle it." What Fen didn't see was that the deputy had already depressed the transmission button on his radio.

"Who said that?" demanded Lori.

The deputy responded in a meek voice. "That's Sheriff Maguire."

The next radio broadcast came from Sgt. Tom Stevens. He began by stating his badge number, followed by, "I'll take over securing the area until a supervisor from the sheriff's office arrives."

"My ETA is twenty minutes. Make sure no one contaminates my crime scene."

Fen rolled his eyes, then directed his attention to the distant rise where two more vehicles from the sheriff's department came with lights flashing. One still had his siren activated. Tom gave instruction to the first deputy to string yellow tape along the wooded river bank for about a hundred yards upstream and downstream.

A sheriff's department lieutenant, new to the department since Fen left, approached and looked down on him. "What's your name?"

"Fen Maguire."

"Your full name," he demanded.

Instead of answering, Fen pulled out his wallet and handed his driver's license to the lieutenant.

After a thorough examination, the lawman raised his gaze to meet Fen's. "So, you're James Fenimore Maguire."

Fen nodded.

With a smirk and a nod, the man said, "I've been looking forward to meeting you."

License in hand, the lieutenant turned and strode to his vehicle.

Fen sighed. His gut told him he and the new sheriff's right-hand man may not see eye-to-eye.

Chapter Two

More emergency vehicles arrived, including volunteer firemen, an ambulance, and three additional deputies. A Toyota Camry also came down the slope into the river valley. It pulled into a field away from the official vehicles. Fen watched the woman exit the car and come toward him.

It had been nine months since he'd last seen her. Still grieving his wife's death at the time, and only days away from his tenure as sheriff ending, he'd not paid much attention to Lou Cooper's looks. He guessed her to be in her early forties. She wore a navy jacket over a light-colored blouse, gray slacks and shoes that could pass for casual. She also had pretty eyes. A little too intense, but pretty all the same.

She scanned the crowd and honed in on the four-wheeler. "Mr. Maguire, it's been a while."

He nodded an affirmative answer. "You still look like a big-city reporter."

"That's because I am, at heart. Since this is your land, do you mind if I take notes?"

"It's fine with me, but this is an active crime scene. Sheriff Newman will be in charge as soon as she arrives."

Fen motioned for the reporter to come closer. She leaned in and he caught a whiff of her perfume. "Don't get too close to any of the first responders and don't ask questions for a while. Some of these deputies are new and don't know to keep their mouths shut. You should get most of what you need by listening."

She whispered back, "Why don't you tell me?"

He grinned through the pain of his knee. "I know better. If I say anything, it will appear in print."

About twenty-five minutes after Lori's last transmission, her voice came over the multitude of radios. She directed the transmission to her lieutenant. "Where is everyone?"

The lieutenant responded, "Didn't the ranch worker tell you where to go?"

"No one's at the gate, only a map. I'm following the directions."

Fen closed his eyes and wondered what Sam had done.

It didn't take long before Lori's sharp voice came over the radio again. "Lieutenant Creech, I'm stuck. Come get me."

"Where are you?"

"How should I know?"

Fen looked at the hapless lieutenant. "Tell her to describe the terrain."

Lori spoke of what sounded like a seldom used path that led to a bog. Fen knew right where she had gone, and it wasn't anywhere near the river. "Tell her to stay in the car. It'll take a tractor to pull her out."

The lieutenant relayed the message.

"I don't have time to wait on a tractor. Come get me now!"

Fen looked up at the lieutenant. "I'll need to show you how

to get there. It's a rough, narrow trail. The four-wheeler is better suited for where we need to go."

The lieutenant shook his head. "From what Sheriff Newman's told me about you, I can't trust you to tell me anything."

Fen shrugged. "Suit yourself. Good luck finding her."

The lieutenant stroked his thick, black mustache. "How 'bout I arrest you for obstructing an investigation?"

Sergeant Stevens took the number of steps necessary to invade the lieutenant's personal space and issued an icy stare. "Back off before your mouth overloads your badge." Without looking away, Tom spoke to Fen. "Where's Sheriff Lori?"

"Blackman's Slough. Not over fifty yards from where you killed that feral hog last winter."

Tom gave the next command. "Your truck, Lieutenant. You'll need a new paint job after today."

Fen watched the two men drive away, then tested his leg and took a few tentative steps while leaning on his hickory cane. Not too bad, but he dreaded the swelling that was sure to follow. He watched from a distance as the men milled about, not knowing what to do until the rescue boat arrived. It was a disorganized mess, but they pulled the lifeless body out of the water and brought it to shore. Most everyone stepped up to view the victim, and because of the condition of the body, backed away with haste.

Judge Stone arrived, put on blue gloves, and motioned for Fen to join him. "Do you know him?"

"Hard to tell. Something about him is familiar."

The justice of the peace asked the paramedics to roll the body over. A gloved hand lifted a soggy shirt as Fen and the judge examined the victim's back. Nothing but a few abrasions. Next, the judge lifted a thatch of mud-stained hair from around the left temple. He continued to pull back the hair at the base of the skull. "Uh-oh. This is a homicide."

Fen closed the distance and stared at a small hole, no larger than the diameter of the pencil he'd been sketching with. "That's not just a homicide; it's an execution."

"No exit wound," said Judge Stone.

Fen looked at the ambulance attendant. "Could you get a towel and clean off the mud from the back of his belt?"

With a few swipes, the belt revealed a hand-tooled name—Clete. Fen blurted out, "Cletus Brumbaugh. I thought he looked familiar."

The announcement brought renewed interest in the body, and people formed a tight circle around him. "Turn him over," came a voice from someone. "Yep. It's Clete, all right."

Fen took out his cell phone, called Tom, and gave him an update.

It wasn't long before Lieutenant Creech's truck barreled across the river valley. After sliding to a stop, a shrill voice overpowered all the others. "Everyone get back."

Like Moses parting the Red Sea, Lori Newman's command caused the first responders to make a path. She took a cursory glance at the body and then fixed her gaze on Fen.

He gave her a quick head-to-foot look. From the knees down, she was nothing but drying mud. She had another brown smudge that went all the way across her forehead and into a lock of sandy-brown hair. Other than a tear on the hip revealing pink panties, her designer dress looked unscathed.

Lori's forehead wrinkled. "Who made this map?" She waved a piece of paper in Fen's face.

He shrugged. "Sam, I guess."

"Then that ex-con's going back to jail where he belongs."

Fen jerked the paper from Lori's hand and gave it a quick

glance before she could take it back. Through gritted teeth, she said, "I'm glad you did that. Now you're going to jail, too."

Fen set his feet shoulder length apart. "Look again, Lori. There's nothing wrong with that map other than you had it upside down."

Snickers and more than a few laughs came from those assembled.

Tom had taken his time joining them. "Sheriff Newman, I need to talk to you."

"What is it?" she snapped.

"You need to go to the boat ramp by the bridge. A state trooper has the area taped off. She believes there's evidence suggesting the boat ramp may be the original crime scene. I told her to call Danni Worth to do the crime scene investigation."

"That wasn't your place."

Tom gave her a fatherly smile and scanned her mud caked legs. "You've been busy, and I only did what you would have done."

Fen wondered if Lori would have remembered to call Danni, or was she so pig-headed that she'd mess up another crime scene? Either way, it wasn't his problem.

While Lori occupied herself by telling her officers what to do, Tom motioned for Fen to step away from the crowd. They moved to the shade of a massive pecan tree, where the sergeant faced the ambulance. "Danni's coming here after she's finished at the boat ramp."

Fen nodded. "There won't be anything to look at but tire tracks and footprints from the first responders."

The corner of Tom's mouth quirked upward. "My guess is, Danni will ask you for a glass of iced tea and a long conversation."

A groan was Fen's only response.

Tom chuckled. "Look. Lori's sending her officers farther downstream. There goes Danni's search area."

Fen shrugged and tried to look disinterested. He would have limited the searchers to one man, Sam. The half-Choctaw Indian knew the difference between trash and something usable in court.

Fen's thoughts then went to Danni Worth. He hadn't seen her since the last homicide he investigated. That was a few months after Sally died and his world stopped spinning. Danni had been too willing to help him grieve.

The ambulance loaded Clete and took off at a slow pace. Fen turned to Tom. "Would you mind asking Lori's lapdog lieutenant for my driver's license? I'm not sure he has any intention of giving it back to me."

Tom nodded. "Things sure ran better when you were sheriff. I hope you're planning on running again."

Fen pointed to the September sun. "I might consider it when that freezes over." He scratched two days' growth of whiskers on his chin. "You're close to retirement. Why don't you throw your hat in the ring?"

Tom didn't reply, which told Fen the highway patrol sergeant had already considered it, but the election wouldn't be for three more years.

While Fen contemplated how he could help Tom get elected, Lori strode toward them. "Mr. Maguire, you'll need to come to the sheriff's office and make a formal statement today."

"I'll be there tomorrow morning."

Lori shook her head with vigor. "You're coming with me today."

"Can't."

"Why not?"

"My attorney doesn't work on Sundays, and I'm not answering questions without him."

While Lori's face reddened, Fen shifted his gaze to her ruined sandals. "I hope you put on bug spray before you came. The chiggers in this Johnson grass are thick this year."

Lori looked down at her bare legs and stomped both feet. Tom took pity on her. "Come with me, Lori. There's nothing else to do here and we should both be at the boat ramp. I'll fill you in on what Fen told me and show you the photos I took."

Lori agreed and took off at a quick pace. Tom hung back and spoke in a soft voice. "Good luck with Danni when she comes calling."

Fen extended a hand and received a firm handshake. "Good luck with Lori. Try to keep her from messing up this case. Few people liked Clete, but he didn't deserve to die the way he did."

Tom nodded in agreement. "Go sit in your farm buggy while I get your driver's license."

Fen's thoughts went to his late wife and then to Danni Worth. He hoped Danni would change her mind about coming to see him.

Chapter Three

By the time Fen cranked the four-wheeler and pointed it toward home, his breakfast had long since left him. Instead of parking in the fourth opening of his garage, he pulled around back and brought the machine to a stop, pointing it toward the pool. He went to the back door, pushed it open, and lifted a foot to take a step inside when a voice boomed from some distance away. "Don't you dare come in with muddy boots!"

He backtracked, hooked the heels of his boots in a boot-jack, and left them outside. Bending over, he put a two-inch cuff on the legs of his jeans to make sure any hitchhiking mud didn't fall on the shining hardwood floor. Thelma Blackwood was particular about housework and cooking. In fact, she had definite opinions about most things.

Once in the kitchen, Fen found Thelma pulling a trove of items from the refrigerator. "I worked like a mule all morning getting this oversized house clean. You're getting a sandwich, chips, and potato salad for lunch."

"You know I'm not particular."

"It's a good thing. If you were, you'd be looking for another gal to take care of you. You're lucky I've stayed as long as I have."

Fen made a mental check mark in his mind. That was the third threat to leave she'd made so far today. Only six or seven more to go before the sun went down. "Did Sam tell you about the body in the river?"

Thelma tented her hands on ample hips. "You know better than to ask me a question like that. That husband of mine barely talks to you, let alone to me." She brought out both mayonnaise and mustard. "That doesn't mean I didn't turn on the scanner in your office and find out on my own. I almost busted a gut when I heard Lori Newman call for help after she got stuck. I love it when karma visits a prissy prima donna like her."

Fen gave Thelma a hard stare.

"Don't be giving me the stink eye for speaking my mind. That woman and her daddy deserve worse than gettin' stuck for the way they treated you after Miss Sally died. If you ask me, the angel of death took the wrong sister, and he should have grabbed Nathaniel Newman, too. Could have gotten a two-for-one deal."

A shiver went through Fen. Then came the contraction in his gut. He spoke as he walked. "I'll be in my office. No lunch today."

Thick curtains muted the sunlight as it tried to break into the office. He liked it dark when he needed to talk to Sally. After closing the door and locking it, he took an urn from a shelf and placed it on a short table in front of his favorite leather chair. He settled in and looked at the brass receptacle holding his wife's ashes. "Sorry I didn't spend more time with you this morning. I wanted to catch the early light for the painting I had in mind to start. That location won't be the same after seeing the body of Clete Brumbaugh. I'll need to find somewhere else." He looked across the room. "Hold on a minute, I'm parched."

Fen went to the mini-fridge, pulled out a bottle of water, and returned to his chair. "The good thing about our talks these days is, you're never in a hurry." He unscrewed the top and drained half of it. "I packed water, but with all the excitement, I didn't think to stay hydrated."

With head leaned back, Fen prepared to tell Sally all about the morning and wait for a response that came only in his imagination. The phone vibrated in the pocket of his shirt. He thought it might be Sam saying either Lori or her lieutenant were booking him on some trumped-up charge. He looked at the screen. It wasn't Sam but Monica Frye, one of Sally's best friends and counselor at the high school.

"It's Monica," he said to the urn. "Should I talk to her?"

Despite his desire not to push the green button on his phone, the nudge to his soul won out. "Hello, Monica."

She bypassed the normal pleasantries. "There are a dozen rumors going around about someone getting killed on your property. I had to call and make sure you're all right."

Normally, Fen wouldn't disclose information on a homicide, but this was Monica and he no longer carried a badge. Not only had she been a trusted friend and confidant to Sally for years, she was an information gatherer—not a gossip, but one who had a knack for listening. The students were lucky to have such a compassionate counselor.

The words tumbled from his lips. "Someone killed Clete Brumbaugh and dumped him in the river. That's where I found him this morning. There's nothing to show he died on our property. The sheriff is concentrating on the boat ramp as the original crime scene."

"I'm relieved." Monica paused. "You're still using *our* instead of *my* property."

"Can't help it."

Monica responded in a way he wasn't expecting. "There's a new girl in school this year, a senior from Houston. She's in Trudy's art class. She says the girl has genuine talent, but has had a rough life and a rotten home environment."

When Fen didn't respond, Monica softened her voice and said, "I think you could make a difference in her life, give her hope. I'm sure Trudy would love to have you speak to her students like you used to. And I miss seeing you here in the halls of the school. You're a natural with those art students."

His throat became so dry he could barely respond. Searching for a reason not to, the best he could come up with was, "Not yet. Maybe in a few months. Maybe after Christmas."

"I understand." She paused. "You have a lot to give, Fen. It's not just the students who would miss out if you don't share what you have."

"I'll give it some thought," Fen croaked out.

With the unexpected call disconnected, Fen got back to his one-sided talk with Sally. "Sorry, honey. I know it's not what you'd do, but going back to that school and passing your classroom would be too much right now."

After a few minutes of silence, he put the urn back in its place. As always, he brought his index finger to his lips, touched it to the urn, and stared at Sally's photos flanking both sides. He wondered again how long the hollow feeling would haunt him.

After easing the door open, he padded his way to the kitchen. Thelma sat at the table in the breakfast nook with hands clasped in prayer and a mound of tissues in front of her.

He cleared his throat and opened the refrigerator door, giving her time to compose herself and throw away the tissues.

"Sheriff, get your head out of that refrigerator. I'll have a sandwich ready for you in two shakes. I made some stuffed celery to tide you over and there's a fresh pitcher of tea."

He didn't correct her for using his former title because it would do no good. "I'm all right now. Dealing with death affects me differently than it used to."

"I guess you and I will keep on talking to Miss Sally for some time to come."

"I can't think of any reason not to if it helps me get by."

Thelma allowed a smile to part her lips. "My momma said I was born with my tongue split right down the middle so I could talk to two people at the same time. That wasn't true, but I don't see any reason I can't talk to the living and those that have passed on. Been doing it all my life."

He spoke over his shoulder. "You need to prepare a little extra for dinner tonight."

"Who are you expecting?"

"Danni Worth, if she finishes processing the crime scenes before the day's too far gone."

Fen looked at Thelma's reflection in the window. She had a knife in her hand and waved it like an orchestra conductor does a baton. "That woman was trailing you even before Miss Sally had her heart transplant. Mark my words; nothing good is going to come of her parking her feet under your table."

"I'm curious about what she found today."

"Why? You're not the sheriff."

"Then why don't you call me Fen?"

"Turn around and I'll tell you."

Fen did as instructed.

"I call you Sheriff because that's who you are and will

always be to me. You and Miss Sally believed in me even though I did all I could to mess up my life."

Fen smiled. "She twisted my arm."

"Horsefeathers. It might have been her idea to take me in after you finished this big house, but you're the type of man that can't help but do what's right."

Fen turned around and stared out the window where he and Sally used to watch the sunrise. "How's that sandwich coming?"

Thelma launched into a monologue about all the bologna sandwiches she made in the county jail's kitchen. Fen tuned her out as she rambled on and shifted his thoughts to wondering what Danni Worth might be finding.

Chapter Four

The western sky had turned a dozen shades of orange and pink when Danni pulled into the circular driveway. Fen peeked out his office window as his guest unzipped, then tugged and shrugged her way out of white bio-hazard coveralls. She wadded them into a ball and pitched them onto the floorboard of the crime scene van. From the passenger's side of the front seat, she dragged out a black gym bag.

Fen pulled the front door open before Danni rang the doorbell. Her hand immediately went over her face. "Don't look at me until I do something with myself. If I remember right, there's a guest bathroom down the hallway to the right."

"It hasn't moved since the last time you were here."

"That's been a long time. I hope you don't mind if I take a quick shower. Believe me, you don't want me in the same room until I make myself presentable."

"Take your time. Thelma put out fresh towels today. There's a hair dryer in the closet."

Danni issued a crooked smile and scurried away. Fen hadn't seen her since Lori took over as sheriff, but she hadn't changed. Her short strawberry-blond hairdo made her face look pudgy. He remembered the high school basketball game when a wild elbow from an opposing player broke her nose. The doctor had done a remarkable job of straightening it. Still, he couldn't help but remember the way she looked in the yearbook with two black eyes. Otherwise, she had the figure of a well-endowed athlete with broad shoulders and an abundance of curves. Sam described her as good breeding stock.

The rattle of pots in the kitchen caught Fen's attention as he strode down the hall to check on Thelma's progress with dinner. She was bent over, checking something in the oven when he arrived. "Danni's taking a shower. She shouldn't be long."

Thelma let out a snort that communicated disbelief and disgust at the same time. She closed the oven door and righted herself. "Supper will hold for half an hour without drying out. After that, she'll take her chances."

"It shouldn't take her long to rinse off."

Thelma wagged her head. "Shows what you don't know about women. Danni ain't like Miss Sally. But then, nobody I ever met had skin like hers and such pretty blond hair. More than that, she enjoyed life so much she didn't waste time primping."

"You won't get an argument from me on any of that, but why do you think it will take Danni over thirty minutes?"

"Like most gals, she's got a wide streak of vanity running through her. Besides that, she wants to set her hook in you and reel you in. It will take her at least half an hour to get her bait ready after she dries off."

Fen used his hand to shoo away Thelma's suspicions. She responded by raising her eyebrows and tilting her head. It was her way of challenging him to a verbal duel. Instead of falling into the trap, he asked for a refill of iced tea. "I'll be in my office."

Thelma's estimation of the time for Danni to shower and put herself together proved accurate. She walked through the open door to Fen's office in a cloud of cloying perfume.

Once inside the sanctum of his office, she moved to a bookcase and examined the selections. "See anything that interests you?" asked Fen.

"You kept your college textbooks." She placed a finger on the spine of a thick tome. "I have this one on photographing crime scenes."

Fen nodded. "I doubt it. That's a first edition. It's gone through revisions since I was in college and you're a lot younger than me. I bet yours is a later edition."

Her gaze shifted to the urn containing Sally's ashes, and she dipped her head. "Sorry. I'm invading a very private space."

He stood. "Go through the living room and onto the back patio. I'll check with Thelma to make sure dinner is ready."

Thelma spoke as soon as Fen entered the kitchen. "I'll need to get the shop fan out of the garage to get the smell of perfume out of the house after she leaves. Bon appetite, or whatever it is those people in France say."

Fen let out a sigh. "Please tell me you didn't poison Danni's food."

"Not enough to do permanent damage." She pointed in the direction of the guest house on the garage side of the pool. "I'll tell her she can join you in the dining room on my way to put my feet up. All that cleaning, cooking, and thinking today wore me out, so I'll leave you and your guest alone. There are two servings of key lime pie in the refrigerator. Before you go to bed, rinse everything and load the dishwasher."

He gave a nod, and they gave each other a fist-bump. It was

their way of acknowledging Thelma was off the clock and not to bother her until tomorrow morning.

Danni sat in front of a plate crowned with a metal cover. Fen took his place at the head of the table and noticed that Thelma had removed the chair to his right, his late wife's place of honor.

As was his custom, Fen dipped his head, offered a brief prayer of thanksgiving for the food and for Thelma's efforts. After a quick "Amen" he managed a weak smile. "Let's dig in."

"Double amen to that. I forgot to restock my go-bag and all I've had to eat today was a pack of orange-colored peanut butter crackers and a fruit roll up." Off came the lid from her plate and her eyes widened. "Prime rib cooked medium rare! I've died and gone to heaven."

Half of Danni's meal was gone before she noticed Fen's plate didn't include the slab of meat. She swallowed hard. "I forgot. You and Sally went vegetarian."

Fen rested his fork on the edge of his plate. "Sort of ironic, isn't it? We have four thousand acres of river valley land, raise cattle, plus corn and grains to feed them. And all I'm eating is vegetables."

"You used to eat meat every meal. Why did you and Sally change?"

"A long time ago, before the transplant, the doctors told Sally it would be better for her heart if she laid off so much red meat. You know how she was. She didn't do anything halfway, so I tagged along. I'm easing back into eating meat, but not much, and not very often."

He pushed away his half-eaten meal of vegetables. "She should have eaten whatever she wanted, for all the good it did." He looked at Danni as she touched a napkin at the corners of her mouth. "I'm sorry. Finish your meal."

Danni placed her napkin beside her plate. "I've had plenty.

It was delicious." She looked at a painting on the wall. "That's a wonderful likeness of Sally."

Fen turned his head. "It's special and took me years to complete. I never could capture her eyes, until near the end."

Danni kept staring at the painting. "She's just as I remember her—the prettiest girl in town."

She ran her fingers down the side of her glass of iced tea. "Do you know Sally and my daddy died on the same day?"

Fen shook his head. "I'm sorry. Your father was a good man." He stared at the painting. "We both lost a lot last year."

Danni modulated the tone of her voice to something with a note of cheer in it. "We found a pistol this afternoon. I sent it to the lab in Austin."

Fen sat up straight and locked his gaze on her. "Where was it? What caliber?"

Danni chuckled and wagged an index finger at him. "I see the old bloodhound in you that wants to get back in the hunt. It's a Ruger 22, and I found it in four feet of water."

"Near the boat launch?"

Danni nodded. "Off to one side."

"Right or left?"

"Right."

Fen pushed his plate away a little farther and rested his forearms on the table. "Did you find anything else?"

"Nothing anywhere near the bridge. I might have picked up some useful footprints near where you fished the body out of the water, but the first responders tromped all over the bank."

Fen held up his hands. "I didn't touch the body in the water or on land."

"What about Sam?" She raised a hand. "Before you tell me he knows nothing about this, I found fresh hoofprints from an unshod horse that started at your property line and went all the way to where you had your easel set up. He galloped off in a big hurry."

Fen took a drink of iced tea. "He trailed Clete floating in the river until the body got tangled in the tree. Does Lori know he was there?"

Danni let out a laugh. "Are you kidding? Lori wouldn't know what to do with that information even if I included it in my report. You should have seen her. She looked like a long-haired dog at a flea and tick convention. She scratched her legs from ankles to the nether regions when she thought people weren't looking. Doesn't she know you don't walk through Johnson grass in late summer wearing a sundress and sandals? Especially with all the rain we had this summer."

Fen couldn't help himself. "It's her punishment for wearing white sandals after Labor Day."

Danni leaned her head back and let loose a riotous laugh. Fen couldn't help but smile, even though the joke was on his former sister-in-law. It was good to hear laughter again in the house.

Fen relaxed, more comfortable with Danni than he expected to be. She didn't seem as pushy as he remembered. He guessed time and maturity had mellowed her enough to where he might sneak in a few questions. "I've been so out of the loop for the past year that I didn't realize Lori hired a new lieutenant. What's the story on him?"

Without hesitating, Danni said, "Lieutenant Jake Creech. He was a patrol sergeant in Falls County."

Fen interrupted. "Are you still covering that county as well?"

"If they need extra help. It's part of a multi-county mutual aid agreement. Of course, the Department of Public Safety will send in a team if it's something extra-big or has political implications."

"I guess Clete Brumbaugh's murder didn't rate high enough for the State of Texas to send anyone."

Danni shook her head. "Dead drug dealers don't raise too many eyebrows. A few columns in the local paper, an autopsy followed by a poorly attended funeral, and a quiet burial. By Halloween, no one will care."

She took a sip of tea. "Back to Lieutenant Creech. It seems he's hitched his wagon to Lori Newman's rising star. There's talk about them getting chummy, if you know what I mean."

Fen pursed his lips and gave his head a nod. "That would explain why he wanted to haul me in today. I'm not in good standing with the new sheriff and her father. Their opinion of me is bound to rub off on Lori's deputies."

Danni gave her head a firm shake. "The deputies you trained will still walk on hot coals for you. It's only the new hires that are being influenced." She lowered her voice. "Don't underestimate Lori's right-hand man. The deputies call him Jake the Snake."

"I can understand why."

Silent moments passed before Fen looked at Danni and squinted. "Why are you really here tonight?"

Danni leaned back and cocked her head. "You have a way of cutting to the chase, Sheriff Maguire."

He lowered his voice. "It's Fen, not Sheriff Maguire."

She chuckled. "Whatever you say."

He stared.

She stared back, leaned forward, and placed her hand on his forearm. "Someone killed a man not more than a mile from your property line. You and I both know that Lori Newman doesn't have a chance of finding who murdered Clete Brumbaugh. It drives both of us crazy if people get away with murder."

Fen stood. "Even if it drives me all the way crazy, I won't

get tired from the trip." He closed his eyes and took in a deep breath. "Listen close. I'm not the sheriff, and I don't carry a badge or a gun anymore."

Danni also stood and tented her hands on her hips. "Then get a badge, put your gun back on, and do what you know is right."

Fen stood and paced. "Even if I wanted to be a cop, I can't pass a physical with this bum knee."

"Who says you have to be a cop?" She gave him a look that telegraphed both frustration and sympathy. "What's happened to that sharp mind? You always got things done when no one else could. There were cases you solved that everyone said were hopeless. You always came through."

He raised his voice. "Then why didn't I save Sally?"

Danni didn't back down. "She decided not to search for another heart. Not you!"

Their words echoed against the dining room walls. He wanted to shove them back into both their mouths. All he could do was walk away and go into his office. Later, he came out to apologize, but the house was empty. She'd put the dining room back to rights, the kitchen was clean, and the dishwasher loaded and running. He'd call her tomorrow and apologize.

In his bathroom, he looked in the mirror and saw the sticky-note, a reminder to go to the sheriff's office the next morning. He moaned, went to his nightstand, and picked up his phone. He dictated a brief message to Lori, telling her he'd be there at 9:00 a.m. The video of Clete floating in the Brazos took off into cyberspace attached to an email.

Once in bed, he concluded that the next day had the potential to be every bit as rotten as this day had been.

Chapter Five

The cell phone in Fen's pocket came to life as he backed his 1972 Ford Bronco from the third stall of the garage. It was the first time he'd driven it in over a month, and it needed some exercise to keep the battery charged. He turned off the engine and allowed it to coast to a stop on the concrete driveway. Looking down, he noticed the familiar name of Trudy Greenwood on the phone's screen.

"Hello, Trudy. How are things at the high school?"

"Fabulous! This is my fourteenth year and it's going to be a special year. I'm sure of it."

In his mind's eye, Fen pictured the five-foot, one-inch art teacher bouncing from student to student, giving encouragement to each. She likely wore garish clothes and a beret over an explosion of curly red hair. "What can I do for you?"

"Well, since you asked." She milked a dramatic pause for several seconds. "I was thinking over the weekend about what would give the students an extra jolt of inspiration. I said to myself, 'Trudy, what famous artist could you get to give a pep talk to the students?' Your name literally flew into my mind as if it had a golden head and iridescent wings. Please, please, please give a talk and a short demonstration on how you begin a painting?"

Fen let out a short groan. "Trudy, you know you don't need me for that. You start with an idea, a pencil and a sketchbook."

The response didn't dissuade her. "You and Sally always had such a special way with the students. It's like magic when you establish perspective and set horizon lines on your works."

The lump in Fen's throat competed with the knot that tied in his gut. "I'm sorry, Trudy. To get to your classroom, I'd have to pass by Sally's. I haven't been able to drive by the school, let alone come into the building."

Trudy's voice lowered. "I understand, but I've also seen many students helped through inevitable teenage emotional swings by the things they create. What's going on inside them works its way out in their sketches. It's therapy that doesn't require words or counseling. Your encouragement helps that process."

With silence on Fen's end, Trudy changed the subject. "Tell me you're painting again."

"I'm getting back to it slowly. In fact, I was sketching a river scene yesterday."

"Is that when you discovered the body?"

Fen blinked twice. "I forgot how quick news travels among high school kids. What are they saying?"

Trudy's voice came forth like a fast-flowing spring. "You know how they are. Their mouths work faster than their brains. Every rumor imaginable is going around."

"Including one that says I killed Clete?"

Trudy responded with uncharacteristic silence.

Fen looked in the rearview mirror. He didn't like the scowl

reflecting at him. "If they think that, they probably believe I killed Sally, too."

Trudy responded with force. "You know better than anyone that these kids play way too many computer games, most of which train their vulnerable minds to think wrong thoughts."

"Yeah, but those kids have parents who talk to other parents. It's the curse of a small town."

"Be positive. This will all blow over when they find the killer."

"You're probably right, but that gives me another reason for not coming to school. Dagger stares and sideways glances wouldn't be good for me, you, or the students."

Trudy let out a huff. "Oh, all right. My timing is off, but I'm counting on you coming back after they make an arrest."

"An arrest and a conviction," said Fen.

"Such a shame," said Trudy. "I have a new girl this year, Bailey Madison. She has such raw talent, but she also has a few strikes against her, not the least of which is that she's the niece of Cletus Brumbaugh. I'll admit she's a bit of a handful, but that's often the mark of genius. She doesn't settle for good enough."

When Fen didn't respond, Trudy asked, "By the way, are you setting up your booth at the Harvest Festival?"

"That's not until mid-October. Right now, I'm living one day at a time. Haven't even considered the festival."

"Then think about it, and think hard. Being around people will do you good. Got to go. Bye."

Fen looked at the face of the phone as the screen changed. "She's like a pit bull. I'll need a good excuse to get out of the Harvest Festival."

He turned the key and brought the Bronco to life. It still ran as smoothly as the day he bought it for Sally as a birthday present. It was already decades old by then, but only had seven hundred and thirty-four miles on it.

Twenty minutes later, he arrived in the parking lot of the sheriff's office. The first two deputies he encountered greeted him with his former title as he stepped toward the door. He cautioned them to be careful and asked if they'd seen Sheriff Newman.

"Called in sick," said a deputy named Salinski. He cupped his left hand around one half of his mouth and lowered his voice. "Doc Brown went to her house last night and treated her for chiggers in places they ought not to have been."

The second deputy made a half-hearted attempt not to laugh.

"I told Lori I'd be here this morning," said Fen. "Who am I supposed to talk to?"

The door opened, and Lieutenant Creech stepped into the parking lot. "I'll take care of this guy."

The two deputies took several steps back. Fen noticed that Deputy Salinski activated his body camera and nudged the other officer to do the same.

Fen turned and made a point of hooking his thumbs in the back pocket of his jeans.

"Put your hands where I can see them," said Lieutenant Creech.

Fen turned around and waved with eight fingers before he spun back around. "No guns, no knives, two witnesses, and, of course, you, Lieutenant Creech. I'm sure you're not threatened by a man who's still a certified peace officer."

"Quit the comedy routine and follow me."

Fen tilted his head. "Why should I follow you? I'm supposed to meet Sheriff Lori."

The muscles in the lieutenant's jaw flexed. "Her name is Sheriff Newman, Maguire, and—"

Fen cut him off. "I prefer to be called Fen. If you think that's too informal, you can call me Mr. Maguire."

"If you don't quit stalling, I'll be calling you Inmate Maguire."

"I didn't realize you were in a hurry. It's a good thing I sent a detailed witness statement to Sheriff Lori last night." He held up a hand. "My bad. Let me rephrase that last sentence. I sent a statement to Sheriff Newman. She and Sergeant Stevens have video of the body in the river and the riverbank before we made tracks down to the water."

"I'm not taking your word for anything."

"I thought you wanted to save time. I do too. Give me your work email address and I'll send you a copy of the statement and the video. If you have any further questions, I can come back after I get a cup of coffee and we'll have a nice, friendly talk."

"I have a better idea," said Creech. "I'll have these two deputies arrest you for failure to cooperate in an investigation and resisting arrest."

Fen turned to Salinski and the other deputy. "You're not obligated to follow an illegal order." He turned back to the lieutenant. "Like I said, I'll be back after I get a cup of coffee. Don't worry about giving me your email address. I already have it."

"You'll regret this, Maguire, and that's a promise."

Fen turned away from the threat, re-hooked his thumbs in his back pockets, and gave an eight-fingered goodbye wave.

From behind him, he heard Lieutenant Creech dressing down the two deputies as they entered the building. Once out of earshot, he took his phone from his shirt pocket and scrolled down the screen until he found the name Chuck Forsythe. A woman answered.

"Candy, it's Fen. Can you put me through to Chuck?"

"Fen," said Chuck. "Candy and I have been talking about

you since we heard about Clete washing up on your property. I was wondering if I should call you."

"Do you have time for a cup of coffee?"

"Stop by my office. There's a fresh pot brewing."

"I'm on my way."

Chapter Six

By the time Fen arrived at the law office of Chuck Forsythe, his knee throbbed to the beat of a marching band's snare drum. Candy met him with open arms and a hug he wasn't sure would end.

When they drew apart, her eyebrows knitted together in worry. "Did you hurt your knee again?"

He nodded. "I made a wrong turn yesterday."

"Let's go to Chuck's office and I'll bring you an ice pack. Are you sure there's nothing they can do to fix it?"

Fen gave a tight-lipped smile which turned into an open mouth grimace when he walked. "Nothing I'm willing to let them do."

Chuck spoke from behind his desk. "Not there, Candy. Put him on the couch so he can elevate that leg. Get that blue ice-pack thing out of the freezer."

She glared at her husband. "You take care of the lawyering, and I'll do the nursing."

Candy left as Fen settled in and Chuck pushed a chair

close so both men could look at each other without twisting their necks.

"It's about time you came to see me."

Several months had passed since Fen conversed with his friend and attorney. There were a few more sprinkles of gray in Chuck's thatch of dark-brown hair, but otherwise he looked fit and ready to run another marathon. "This visit is part social, but mainly business. You'd better start the clock if you want to get paid."

"Does this visit have to do with Clete Brumbaugh's death?"

"Yes and no. This morning, it has more to do with Lori and her new lieutenant." Fen made a quick scan of the office. "I should probably include Nathaniel Newman in the mix."

"Is he cooking up some kind of scheme to get the land back?"

Fen shook his head. "Not that I know of. In fact, I've not seen or heard from him since Lori became sheriff." Fen paused. "Of course, that doesn't mean he hasn't been plotting to do me harm."

Chuck let out a long sigh of exasperation. "Some people believe money can buy anything. I would have thought he'd mellowed by now."

"Perhaps he will, but for now, he has Sheriff Lori gunning for me, and so is Lieutenant Jake Creech."

"Nathaniel Newman is a crafty old codger." Chuck leaned back. "Speaking of the new lieutenant, I'm hearing bad things about him. Did you have a run-in with him yesterday?"

Fen nodded. "Yesterday and today, with one more planned as soon as I leave here. That's why I came to see you."

Candy knocked on the door and entered, carrying two blue ice packs. She wasted no time in placing a thin towel over Fen's knee, followed by the cold packs.

"Sugar," said Chuck. "Tell Denise to hold all calls. I need you to take notes."

Candy headed for the door without a word as Fen took stock of the attractive brunette two inches taller than Chuck.

"You did well when you talked Candy into marrying you," said Fen. "It's not every lawyer who gets a registered nurse and a paralegal all wrapped up in a good-looking wife."

"We both married up."

Candy returned with a legal pad and pen in hand. By this time, Chuck had placed a second chair beside his. He folded his hands. "Tell me about yesterday and leave nothing out."

"I'll tell you and show you." Fen gave a line-by-line account of his actions from the time he drove to the river and set up his easel until he sent the witness statement and video to Lori. He then recounted today's events and played the audio recording he made of the encounter with Lieutenant Creech in the parking lot.

Chuck asked, "Does Creech know you recorded him?"

"It was in the parking lot, which is public access. I didn't see any reason to tell him."

"Good. Don't tell anyone about it. That will be our ace in the hole if push comes to shove."

"One more thing," said Fen. "I'm almost positive the two deputies turned on their body cameras when Creech started giving me a hard time."

Chuck was now in full lawyer mode, leaning forward and hanging on every word. "I'll submit a demand for the recordings."

"I'd prefer not to get Lori involved. She doesn't have any business being sheriff, but I still count her as my sister-in-law."

Chuck shook his head. "Lori didn't have to run for sheriff, but she did, and now she's responsible for the people who work there. What's on the tapes isn't just for you. From what I'm hearing about Creech, he's running off the good deputies and bringing on deadbeats. More than one deputy has come to me about him."

The attorney stood and stretched. "We still haven't had coffee."

Candy took the ice packs from Fen's knee. "Feeling better?"

He nodded. "Much better. Thanks."

"Be sure to rest it as much as you can. You know the drill. Twenty minutes cold pack on, then twenty minutes off."

They made small talk about how the corn crop came in with near record yields until Candy returned. Fen took his first sip and gave a nod of approval. "I may have to drop in just to get your coffee."

Candy pointed to Fen's mug. "That's my secret. Coffee tastes best if you drink it from a special mug."

Fen held it up. A photo of him and Sally wrapped halfway around the mug. Both of them smiled so widely they looked like cartoon characters. He turned the mug around and read the election results from his first run for sheriff. He'd outdistanced his opponent by a six to one margin.

His journey into fond memories of years gone by ended when Chuck said, "We need to discuss how to handle Lieutenant Creech."

"I told him I'd be back to talk to him."

"What did you plan on telling him that you haven't already stated in your report or shown him on the video?"

"Nothing."

"Then don't go. I'll call him."

Fen flexed his knee and regretted not driving his Bronco to Chuck's office. "Do what you think is best."

Chuck moved behind his desk and picked up his phone. "I'll record the call and put it on speaker so you can hear." He went through all the motions until the voice of Jake Creech came on the line.

"Lieutenant Creech."

"Good morning, Lieutenant. This is Chuck Forsythe. I'm calling to let you know my client, Mr. Maguire, has aggravated an injury to his knee and won't be able to come to your office today."

"That's not acceptable. Sheriff Newman told me to get a witness statement from him."

"When did she tell you that?"

"Yesterday afternoon."

"Wasn't that before Mr. Maguire provided her with a statement and a video of the body in the water?"

"Yeah, but—"

"And didn't Mr. Maguire already email you those things?"

"I'm following orders."

The clipped response told Fen that Lieutenant Creech didn't want to lose this argument.

"Mr. Maguire has fully complied with the wishes of Sheriff Newman."

"I'll be the judge of that, not some hot-shot lawyer."

Chuck took a drink of coffee and took his time lowering his cup. "Lieutenant Creech, you may not know this, but Mr. Maguire is a ten-year veteran of the highway patrol and served as sheriff of this county for nine years. His leadership, skill, and knowledge brought the department that currently employs you out of the dark ages. In fact, he wrote the manual to train officers. He also standardized the witness statement form to exceed legal requirements."

"That may be, but I have questions for him that arise from the video and the statement he made."

"Have you read the portion of the sheriff's department manual pertaining to witness statements?"

"I don't care what it says. He's coming to my office today."

"Are you prepared to arrest him? If so, can you clearly articulate a violation of any law he's violated? Are you aware that under the law, Mr. Maguire is not obligated to assist you with your investigation?"

"Are you saying he's refusing to cooperate?"

Chuck slowed his speech and decreased the volume down to something suitable for a public library. "What I'm trying to explain is, my client has already cooperated." He took another quick sip of coffee. "However, in the spirit of cooperation, my client will address any questions you may have. Submit those to me in writing, and I'll make arrangements for Mr. Maguire to provide answers in a timely manner."

The call disconnected.

Fen stood. "Thanks, Chuck. I'm not sure I'd have been that diplomatic."

Candy put her chair back in its place. "Do you need a ride?"

"That would be best. Concrete sidewalks aren't my friend today, and I don't want Creech towing my Bronco before I can get to it."

Chuck laughed. "It's good to see you can still think like a criminal. It might be a good idea to lie low for a while."

Fen showed him an upraised palm. "I'm going home and will have everything I need delivered for the next month."

"That's good for now, but you can't stay holed up forever. What's your plan for a new normal?"

"I'm thinking about setting up my booth at the Harvest Festival."

Candy's smile made her eyes sparkle. "That's wonderful. Do you have any recent works to show?"

"A few, but they're rather gloomy." Fen looked at his mug once more. "I'm not ready to face many people, but some things happened yesterday that showed me I need people I can trust in my life. Instead of going out to eat this coming Saturday evening, could you two see your way clear to come to the farm? I'll have Thelma fix something special for you."

Chuck extended a hand to help Fen rise as Candy said, "I told Chuck it was best to wait until you did the asking. Of course, we'll be there."

"Thanks for everything, and send me a bill for today."

"That's one bill you'll be waiting a long time to receive." Chuck rubbed his hands together. "About as long as it will take me to respond to questions, if Creech sends them."

Chapter Seven

Three days later, a combination of rest, ice, and over-the-counter anti-inflammatory pills had Fen's knee functioning again. As long as there wasn't a drastic change in the weather or he didn't twist it, his knee functioned at ninety percent of its former capacity. Today had been a good day of painting with almost no pain, even though he stood for two hours. The other four hours he'd spent on a stool, allowing the mixing and application of paint on canvas to minister to his soul.

It was early evening when highway patrol sergeant Tom Stevens came through the back door and onto the patio. Fen waved for the uniformed trooper to join him as he tore off another sheet from the pad and touched it to the flames of a fire pit.

"Isn't it a little hot to sit around the campfire?" asked Tom.

"I'm burning memories." Fen tore off two more sheets and committed them to the flames. "I drew these six days after Sally's memorial service. It was the day my former father-in-law served civil action against me for having Sally cremated."

"I thought that lawsuit took place before she died."

Fen nodded. "That was the first time Judge Rawlings ruled against him. I made these sketches the second time he filed."

Both men stared at the flames and kept silent until Fen unburdened himself of more of his past. He turned. "Let's get some iced tea and you can tell me what's on your mind."

As if he'd already summoned her, Thelma arrived with two tall glasses filled to an eighth of an inch of the brim with amber liquid and clear cubes of ice. "Before you ask, they're both sweet with a wedge of lemon," said Thelma. "Everyone knows that's the way tea ought to be."

Both men thanked the cook/housekeeper and settled in padded lawn chairs. Fen broke the silence by asking, "Are you on duty?"

"Not for another thirty minutes. Thought I'd stop by and check on your knee."

"Much improved. Now tell me why you're really here."

A hint of a smile passed across Tom's face and was gone. "What if I told you I wanted the best glass of iced tea anywhere in the county?"

"I'd say you're right, but there's something else on your mind."

Tom chuckled. "You still have that sixth sense. It served you well when you were sheriff. I'm wondering if you heard about the arrest yesterday afternoon?"

Fen cocked his head. "I haven't heard about it, but what's so unusual about an arrest?"

"It came about because of a tip from an anonymous phone call to DPS in Austin. We traced it to a burner phone. The informant told us where to find several ounces of cocaine."

Tom raised his glass for a drink, giving Fen a chance to ask, "Was it someone I know?"

The glass came down. "He's local. The name we received is your closest neighbor."

Fen jerked forward. "Are you saying they caught the sheriff's father with drugs?"

"Not Mr. Newman, but they were in the back seat of his pickup truck, under a floor mat. Ranch hand Sergio Pena took Mr. Newman's truck to town for routine maintenance. I thought it was Mr. Newman driving and pulled him over. K-9 alerted and there was a pill bottle filled with a white powder. A field test showed it to be cocaine."

Fen leaned back. "Nathaniel Newman wouldn't know cocaine from foot powder." He lifted his gaze to the river in the distance. "Sergio might have a cold beer now and then, but I don't see him messing with anything hard, like cocaine. This smells like a setup to me."

"That's what I think, too, but I had to arrest Sergio all the same." Tom leaned forward and his leather gun belt creaked. "There's more. The caller told us not to let the sheriff's office in on the phone call that tipped us off."

Fen closed his eyes and considered the facts set before him. "Let me go over what you've said so far. An anonymous phone tip came to DPS."

Tom nodded. "To state headquarters in Austin."

"And the caller specifically named Mr. Newman?"

Another nod.

"And it was a coincidence that Sergio was driving instead of the sheriff's father?"

"That's the way I read it."

Fen opened his eyes. "Someone's trying to ruin the reputation of my former father-in-law, but the plan didn't work. Sergio Pena is collateral damage."

"He's already out on bond. Sheriff Lori is fit to be tied because we acted without her knowledge."

Fen processed this additional information and directed a steely gaze at Tom. "You didn't just happen by today."

"What makes you say that?" Tom took another quick drink.

Fen stood and paced a path on the patio while keeping his gaze fixed on the highway patrolman. "If I were in your boots, I'd be looking for someone who had something against Nathaniel Newman. That list is long, but I'm at the top of it. Everyone knows he blames me for Sally's death and it would only be natural that I'd want to strike back for all the things he's done to me." Fen came to a complete stop. "You're here to see if I put cocaine in Mr. Newman's truck."

"For the record, did you?"

"I haven't left the house for three days. Security footage will prove it."

"I don't need it, but it might be a good idea to make sure Chuck Forsythe has it. Any idea who planted the cocaine?"

Fen shook his head from side to side. A thought clicked in his mind. "I believe there's a connection between the murder of Clete Brumbaugh and the drugs found in Mr. Newman's truck. I don't have any idea what it could be, but there's never been a crime connected with Newman land or mine. For two to take place in less than a week, is too much of a coincidence."

Tom leaned forward. "It took me a sleepless night to come up with that idea. You thought of it in a matter of seconds."

After resettling in the chair next to Tom, Fen looked at his friend. "The important thing is that you thought of it. You'll make a fine sheriff after you retire."

Tom shrugged off the compliment. "After Lori is through ruining the department you built, you're bound to be sheriff again."

Fen lowered his voice and spoke in a monotone while looking to the river. "I'll never be sheriff of this county again. Too many memories. I'm not sure what I'll do besides paint, but it won't be sheriff." He turned to Tom. "Could you leave the highway patrol and step into the job if Lori resigns?"

"I could, but she's still in year one of a four-year term. Also, her daddy's already shown he can buy enough votes to get what he wants."

Fen's mind raced with possibilities of what might happen in the present that would affect the future. Instead of giving voice to these, he decided he'd ponder them while he painted. That's when clarity often came to him.

Tom placed his empty glass on the table in front of them. "One more thing. The results of the autopsy came back. Nothing you didn't already know about except the tox screen showed significant amounts of alcohol and barbiturates. Clete couldn't have put up much of a fight."

Fen responded with a non-committal grunt, then volunteered some information of his own. "I'm setting up my booth at the Harvest Festival."

"That's great news. Carrie told me to bring you in at gunpoint if you tried to skip another year. She's nuts about your paintings, but likes the caricature sketches you do of the kids even more."

"Well, I think it's time I got back among the living again and that's as good a place to start as any. We'll see how it goes."

Both men stood, shook hands, and turned their heads as Thelma opened the door. "Mr. Fen, did you leave a message on social media that you were receiving guests tonight?"

"You know I quit social media last year. Do you know who it is?"

Thelma issued a scowl. "I know, and I don't mind telling you, I don't like it one bit. It's that woman who's trying to slide into the spot at the dinner table left by Miss Sally."

"Danni Worth?"

"None other, and I hope you don't expect me to smile when

I send her back here. I don't want that perfume she wears stinking up the house after I cleaned it today."

Tom chuckled, and Fen's eyes rolled skyward. "Be nice and see if she's thirsty."

"I'll give her water."

Fen gave her a hard stare.

"All right, I'll offer her tea, but I'm drawing the line at her putting her feet under the table again."

Tom came to the rescue as the doorbell sounded. "I'll answer that and walk her through the house." He picked up his glass.

"Hand me that," said Thelma. "You're one of my favorites, so don't get on my bad side by trying to take my job from me."

Chapter Eight

"I told Thelma to bring you something tall, cold, and wet," said Fen, as Danni Worth came through the French doors and onto the back patio. He looked past her. "Did Tom leave?"

"I told him I'd been here enough times that I didn't need an escort." She plopped down on the seat recently vacated by the highway patrol sergeant and looked quizzically at the smoldering ashes in the fire pit. "Are you destroying evidence?"

"Something like that." He pointed. "I made these sketches the week after Sally died."

"I've heard of art therapy with kids who undergo traumatic events. I guess it works with adults, too." She paused. "Are you finding burning memories beneficial?"

Fen had reached his daily quota of talking about grief, so he didn't respond. In a stroke of good fortune, Thelma chose that moment to push open the back door and deliver a glass of iced tea to Danni. It came in an insulated tumbler with a wrap-around photo of Fen and Sally and the word *Cozumel* emblazoned across the top in crooked, primary colors. Both wore bathing suits and were toasting each other with drinks crowned with tiny umbrellas.

The door shut behind Thelma as Danni spun the glass around, looking at the photo. She took a sip and cast her gaze over the Brazos River Valley. "You can tell Thelma I'm not trying to take Sally's place."

"I've already told her, but she's stubborn as an old mule looking at an unfamiliar field to plow. It might help if you'd marry someone."

Danni turned to him and wagged her head. "It wouldn't take her long to determine I had a terrible marriage and was hunting for a new, rich husband."

"You're probably right." He looked at the verdant trees along the distant riverbank. "She's loyal as a ten-year old hound and believes it's her duty to Sally to make sure I don't get caught in the snare of a scheming woman." He turned to her. "Don't take it personal. Thelma goes off on a tangent if I mention the name of any woman... single, married, divorced, or anything in between. Come to think of it, she's not too fond of most men, either."

A voice came from over Fen's shoulder. He jerked his head around so fast the popping of his neck brought to mind an adjustment from his chiropractor.

"Sam," shouted Fen, "I'm just now getting over a wrenched knee, and now you're trying to wring my neck. Can't you for once not come up on my blind side?"

Danni covered her mouth as she shook from her belly to her neck.

Sam shrugged the chastisement off like he hadn't heard it. "You have an old mama cow that needs to go to market. I wanted you to know before I took her tomorrow."

"I thought you already culled and replaced all the breeding stock this spring."

"I gave this one another year to drop a calf. That's two years in a row, and she's developed cancer in her eye."

Fen looked up at Sam. "You didn't need my permission to take her."

"The cow's the one Sally named Buttercup."

Fen tried to clear his throat, but it felt like a wad of lint was stuck there. He waved his hand in a way that communicated to Sam to take care of it. The cow would go in the morning, but the memory of Sally bottle feeding the calf lingered. Both Sam and he had written off the orphan calf as beyond hope. Sally loved it back to life.

Sam took soundless steps across the patio, heading to the same dwelling that Thelma walked to every night. Danni turned and spoke in a voice so soft Fen had to concentrate on the words. "I thought Sam lived in a shelter in the woods."

Fen cleared his throat and mind enough to form coherent sentences. "He does most of the time. In fact, he has several huts he stays in." Fen pointed to the smaller house behind the garage. "See that porch light burning?"

"Uh-huh."

"That's Thelma's signal to Sam that she'd like his company tonight."

Danni's hand came over her mouth as she let out a laugh that sounded like a cackle. She lowered her volume and her hand. "I never would have guessed."

"Why not? They're married."

Danni's eyes opened wide in wonder. "Are you kidding me? I'm surprised they ever talk to each other."

"It's one of the great mysteries of life."

"Are you telling me they're married and never speak to each other?"

"The only time I ever heard them exchange words was the day they took me and Sally down by the river and a wrinkled old Indian in full costume conducted their ceremony. We couldn't understand a word he said, and I'm not sure Thelma did either, but the chief had them sign a marriage license and it's filed at the courthouse."

Danni shook her head in disbelief. "I don't surprise easy, but those two together defy all reason. I had them pegged as not liking each other."

"They don't, as far as I can tell." He paused and allowed a smile to lift both corners of his mouth. "Who knows? They may start a trend that reduces divorce by seventy percent."

The subject of Sam and Thelma's relationship had reached a conclusion, so Fen changed the topic. "What's the latest on the murder?"

Danni turned her head and pivoted on the chair to give a full view of her face. "Did Tom give you a report on the autopsy?"

"He said they found alcohol and barbiturates in Clete's system, but he didn't give quantities."

"It was enough to render him unconscious."

"What about the pistol you fished out of the river?"

"Registered to Lori Newman. The bullet that killed him is a match for that gun. Texas Rangers have already questioned her."

They both sat in silence for almost a minute before Danni spoke. "I think somebody's trying to set Lori up. You must have some thoughts about what's going on."

Fen kept his gaze fixed on the spot where he'd set up his easel the morning he spotted Clete's body in the river. "I've known Lori ever since I moved to Springdale when I was a freshman in high school. Sally and I were in the same grade, and Lori was in middle school. She's spoiled rotten, and has her share of character flaws, but she's not a killer. You're right about somebody trying to set her up."

"What are you going to do about it?"

The question drew Fen's focus away from the river. "You're asking the wrong guy. In case you forgot, I no longer carry a badge, or a gun, and I'm not going to."

"That's hard to believe. You were the best sheriff this county ever had, and you know it."

"That's debatable, and it doesn't matter." He pointed toward the tree line of the Brazos. "Take a good look at the river when you pass over it. The water is flowing toward the Gulf of Mexico. It's not backing up. That's how my life has to be or I'll go crazy. I'd give anything and everything I have to make time turn around, but just like that river flows in one direction, that's what my life must do."

"And what happens to Lori if the Rangers hang a murder charge on her?"

He shrugged again. "As things stand now, there's not enough evidence for them to make anything stick. She has position, reputation, and daddy's money to keep her out of trouble. The worst thing that could happen to her is public opinion would force her to resign. Come to think of it, that would be the best thing for her, and the county."

Danni raised her glass. "I'll drink to that." She took a full drink. "But who would take her place?"

"That's four steps ahead on the chessboard. I only think to three. Too many variables and unexpected events to consider."

Fen's gaze went back to the river as Danni took another drink and settled the tumbler on the table in front of her. She spoke as a warm breeze swept across the valley below and rustled the leaves in the trees flanking the porch. "Did Tom tell you about him arresting Sergio Pena yesterday?"

"He told me."

"And?"

"That's what convinced me someone is trying too hard to run Lori off."

"What do you mean?"

"Patterns. Crimes have a way of following patterns. What I'm seeing are anomalies. There's never been a body found at or near the property that belongs to Mr. Newman or this property. There's no history of an arrest for drugs anywhere on or near Mr. Newman's property. That includes his vehicles. He doesn't do drugs, nor does Sergio Pena. Finally, there's never been an anonymous tip sent to DPS headquarters in Austin related to drugs in this county. Whoever is behind this attempt to get Lori's job is leaving too many footprints."

A nod of Danni's head showed she understood and agreed. "What should the person who's behind this do?"

Fen chuckled. "Now you're asking me to think like I'm the bad guy."

"You were always good at that."

"I'm not sure that's a compliment, but to answer your question, if I were the bad guy, I'd lie low for a while. Let things take their course and see how Lori and her father react. It could be the bad guys have already done enough to run her off."

Danni scooted to the edge of her seat with her hands on the arms of the chair. Fen held out his hand to stop her from rising. "Before you go, what's your opinion of Lori's new right-hand man?"

She settled back and made circles with her finger on the arm of the chair. "My vote is still out on him, even though I've known him for several years. He did a good enough job before he came to us from Falls County, but he was a patrolman, not a supervisor. He can follow orders, but it seems Lori's promoted him beyond his capabilities. I've heard rumors that he and Sheriff Lori are getting serious, but you know how rumors go."

Fen nodded. "I'm trying to stay away from him. He gets a

burr under his saddle blanket whenever he sees me." He looked away. "It may not be all his fault. There's something about him that gets under my skin, too. I might have overreacted to the way he talked to me."

Danni stood. "He probably wants to see Lori succeed and doesn't realize she's short on what it takes to be a sheriff. You know what they say about love being blind."

Fen also stood. "You're probably right."

He put a bright tone to his next words. "Any problems I have with Lieutenant Creech will go away with time. In fact, I'm going to be busy here at home finishing a few paintings for the Harvest Festival."

Danny placed her hand on Fen's arm. "You made my day. The festival wasn't the same last year without you. Are you going to draw caricatures of the kids like you always do?"

Fen shook his head. "Sally always took care of the customers interested in my paintings while I drew for the kids. I don't see how I can do both."

"You'll figure out a way."

Chapter Nine

First light pushed away the darkness as Fen pulled his pickup truck, with its custom shell covering the bed, next to the space he'd reserved at the annual Harvest Festival. As always, setup morning was a beehive of activity, with vendors unloading and erecting booths of various sizes. Spirits ran high as artisans socialized, drank coffee, and talked about padding their bank accounts.

He'd thought about asking Sam or Thelma to come with him to help, but their aversion to crowds changed his mind. It taxed both of them to come to town for everyday shopping, let alone be around crowds.

He unloaded and put up a white tent twice the size of what most vendors brought. He affixed special horizontal bracing between the poles that contained rows of hooks, capable of holding paintings of various sizes and weights. By the time he unloaded tables and a lawn chair, sweat rolled off his chin.

One by one, he slid paintings from custom racks in the truck's bed. Each year he had in mind what order they'd hang, but it never worked out to Sally's liking. She'd move them throughout the day, especially when one sold and she'd retrieve a replacement. He was still thinking of her when he unloaded sketch pads and an assortment of artist's pencils. He shook his head when he realized what he held. There'd be no time this year for caricatures and he stowed them under the table.

A jovial man selling handmade pocket knives sat in a lawn chair next to his tent. Fen asked him to keep an eye on things as he went to park his truck and change into a clean shirt.

When he arrived back at his temporary place of business, the pocket-knife man was nowhere to be seen, but that wasn't what brought his long strides to a stop.

"Get your hands off me," came a voice from inside Fen's tent.

"Stop resisting, or you'll get another charge."

The man's voice sounded familiar, and in two more steps Fen understood why. Lieutenant Jake Creech was affixing handcuffs on a young woman. She had long blond hair, parted down the middle. He took another look and noticed her hair had a florescent-green streak running down the right side. She wore paint-stained jeans, a white T-shirt in similar condition, and flip-flops.

"What's going on?" asked Fen in a calm voice.

Creech spun to face him. "This girl was stealing from your booth." He pointed to a stack of sketchbooks and pencils on the table.

Fen gazed at the girl, who squinted at her captor in defiance, her jaw set like a block of granite.

He gave her a wink with the eye away from Creech and pointed at her shirt. "I'm looking at a shirt stained with acrylic paint. There's cadmium red, phthalo green, cadmium yellow, titanium white, and burnt umber. Of course, they've blended to form various shades."

"So what?" said Creech. "You left, and I caught her red-handed trying to take things from under the table."

"I can't see her hands, but I doubt they're red. The only red I see is on her jeans. Besides, she's my helper today."

Creech hooked his thumbs on his gun belt. "If she's your helper, then you know her name. She won't give it to me."

"That's because you're rude. My name is—"

Fen took a stab and hoped he was right. "Her name is Bailey Madison, and she's in Trudy Greenwood's high school art class."

Bailey's eyes grew wide, but only for a moment. "My driver's license is in my back pocket, if you don't believe him."

"Turn around," said Creech.

"I wouldn't do that if I were you, Lieutenant," said Fen. "It's called inappropriate touching, and Miss Madison is particular about that sort of thing."

Bailey maneuvered the handcuffs enough to where she grasped the license. She extracted it from the tight jeans and spun to give it to Creech.

He examined it and said, "This is a Houston address. Where do you live?"

She clamped her mouth shut.

Fen spoke for her. "It's obvious she's done nothing wrong. Please remove the handcuffs."

"Not until she gives me her address and phone number."

The voice of attorney Chuck Forsythe came from behind Fen. "You don't have to give your address and phone number if you don't want to."

Creech spun, his hand gripping his pistol. Chuck didn't seem impressed. "I've been listening to this conversation, and I believe Mr. Maguire's helper has been detained long enough. If you continue to harass my client by delaying the opening of his booth, I'll seek a formal remedy."

Bailey turned around and held out her handcuffs for Creech to take them off. She looked over her shoulder. "Watch what you're touching back there."

Creech set his jaw and made no move to remove the restraints. "It seems I've misplaced my handcuff key. I'll send a deputy around."

"No need," said Fen. "I still have one on my key ring." With practiced efficiency, he slid the silver key in an opening, twisted it, and one side of the handcuffs opened. A repeat of the operation freed Bailey. He ratcheted the cuffs back together and handed them to their owner.

Creech leaned forward and whispered, "That's twice, and I'm keeping score."

Fen issued a toothy grin. "Thanks for being so diligent in looking after my booth."

Everyone waited in place until Creech was well out of sight. Bailey issued a half-hearted word of thanks and took a step. Fen moved in front of her. "Just a minute, young lady. We need to have a quick chat."

She rolled her eyes. "You didn't have to do anything. I could have handled that hick."

"Do you think so? He still has your driver's license, and my guess is he's running a 10-29 on you."

"What's that?"

"He's checking to see if you have any outstanding warrants. Do you?"

"Not anymore. All my run-ins with the law happened before I turned seventeen." She looked in the direction Creech walked.

"Don't even think about it," said Fen. "He shoved your license in the front pocket of his pants. There's no way you can get it without him putting cuffs on you again."

She looked at Fen and then at Chuck Forsythe. "What am I

supposed to do about getting it back?"

Chuck fielded this question. "Handle it by reporting it as lost. You need to change your address while you're on the Department of Public Safety website."

Fen added. "It's probably a blessing that he kept it. If he saw you driving, he might find a reason to pull you over and give you a ticket."

Bailey shrugged. "It doesn't matter. I don't have a car of my own to drive."

"We're two miles outside of town. How did you get here?"

"Thumbed a ride."

Chuck placed his hand on Fen's shoulder. "If you don't need me any longer, I'm going to find Candy before she buys more than I can pay for."

"Hold up a minute. Bailey and I need to go to my truck and get something else."

"I don't think so," said Bailey.

Fen pushed his baseball cap up an inch. "How would you like to earn a couple hundred bucks today?"

Her head tilted like a kitten looking at her reflection in a mirror for the first time. "Doing what?"

"Drawing sketches—caricatures of children, and some adults. It's something I do every year, but I always had my wife to sell the paintings."

Bailey made a scoffing sound. "Your wife? Did she leave you?"

Chuck let out a groan as Fen swallowed and whispered, "Yes. She left me."

"Bummer." She shoved her hands in her jeans. "Before I agree to anything, I want details. What's expected of me? Is this a by-the-hour job, or commission only? How long do you expect me to work? Are you going to pay in cash or check? I have a PayPal account, but I didn't bring my credit card reader."

Fen turned to Chuck. "There's paper on the table. Draw up a contract for both of us to sign. I'm going to get another chair and easel for Bailey. Commission only. She gets all the proceeds from her sales minus the cost of however many sketch pads and pencils she goes through. Children's sketches are free to the customers but I'll pay half the going rate. I'd pay for her lunch and drinks, too, but I'm sure she's too stubborn to accept handouts."

"I didn't say that," countered Bailey.

"I hear you have talent, so earning your own money shouldn't be a problem."

Chuck said, "This won't take me but a few minutes. How long will you be gone?"

Fen spoke over his shoulder. "Bailey stays here with you. Leave whenever you're finished, but make sure she signs it."

Several people stopped Fen on the way back to the booth, so it took him the better part of thirty minutes to return with a chair and an easel. He placed them in the awning's shade at the entrance of his booth. He also brought a sign that read:

FREE SKETCHES
HIGH SCHOOL AND UNDER.
ALL OTHERS $25.00.

Bailey read the sign and sighed. "I almost left when that lawyer told me I'd be working mostly for half-rate."

"You'll be glad you didn't. I'll pay you twelve-fifty each for children's caricatures. Practice speed on them, and don't use colors. Take at least twice as long on the others and give the people their money's worth. Use at least three colors."

She wrinkled her nose in a way that gave him chills. Sally had a habit of doing the same. "Fifteen bucks on the children's sketches."

"Ten dollars."

Her eyes widened. "You said twelve-fifty."

"That will teach you not to get greedy. It's twelve-fifty or hit the road."

She stuck out a hand dappled with paint. "Deal."

Fen shook it, and a jolt went through him. "Deal," he croaked. How many times had he and Sally come to an agreement on something and sealed it with the same word?

He came out of a trance when Bailey spoke, but he didn't catch what she said. "Huh?" was all he could manage.

"I asked if you had any tips for drawing caricatures?"

"Yeah. Exaggerate some part of the body and put the person doing some sort of action. Be careful not to over-exaggerate and offend the customer, especially women."

"What if their backside is wide as this table?"

"Draw them with big heads and small bodies. Don't make enemies out of customers."

She pulled her hair back into a ponytail and secured it with a scrunchy drawn from her jeans. For the first time, he noticed how small and frail she looked. She couldn't have been more than five two, which put him a full foot taller.

"That lawyer told me your wife didn't run off. I'm sorry for what I said. Did you do the painting of her at school?"

Fen nodded.

"I hope someday I can paint like that."

He pointed to the easel he'd set up for her. "Your first customer is waiting."

Sparkling lights came on in her eyes as she spun around to see a chubby baby in his mother's arms. "Well, hi, there, handsome. I bet your momma wants a souvenir of your first visit to the Harvest Festival."

Fen nodded his approval.

Chapter Ten

Bright sunshine gave way to high clouds, making it perfect weather for people to spend the day, and their money, at the Harvest Festival. Fen sold three paintings by ten o'clock, and Bailey's line of customers never dipped below six people waiting. From time to time, he shifted his gaze to the young artist and nodded his approval, even though she had her back to him.

Candy Forsythe paid a visit right after he'd sold his fourth work, another of his older landscapes of the river valley during the cotton harvest. She spent the first few minutes pretending to look at his paintings, but Fen soon realized she was there to watch Bailey work.

"She's good," whispered Candy as Fen sidled next to her. "Chuck told me how you saved her from jail." Her eyes misted over. "You're a good man, Fen."

"Not that good. If it had been anyone but Lieutenant Creech arresting her, I wouldn't have interfered."

"I don't believe that for a minute. If you were still sheriff, there's no way you'd put a girl like that in handcuffs for stealing paper and pencils on the day of the Harvest Festival."

"You're probably right, but as they say, there's a new sheriff in town."

Candy turned enough to take another look at Bailey making swift, sure stokes on paper. "She reminds me of Sally, the way she sits with her back straight."

"Different personalities." Fen shoved his hands in the pockets of his jeans. "She's a tough city girl with a chip on her shoulder the size of a yule log."

"There's nothing wrong with her that a good dose of caring won't cure."

Fen held out his hand toward Bailey. "If you want a project, there she is."

Candy shook her head while still looking at Bailey. "She found you, not me. It's funny the way things get plopped in our laps when we're not expecting them, or even wanting them. Sometimes they turn out to be blessings in disguise."

Before Fen could offer a full-throated denial of any desire to get involved with a troubled teen from the mean streets of Houston, Candy asked, "Has she had anything to eat or drink today?"

"Beats me."

She spun and looked up at him with eyelids narrowed. "What do you mean, you don't know? Do you expect that poor child to slave all day without food or something to drink? Look at her, she's skinny as a broomweed."

Fen pulled a wad of bills from his pocket. "Here. Go get her whatever she wants. I can't leave the booth."

"Keep your money. You'll need it to take her out for supper." Candy glanced past him to the collection of paintings. "I'm surprised you're selling anything, as gloomy as these new ones are."

Candy left to procure food and drink for Bailey. He realized the marked difference between his light-filled earlier works and those he painted after Sally rejected her heart transplant. A funk covered him like a damp blanket, but throngs of customers came with waves of questions. They swept away what could have been a dreary second half of the morning. Another painting sold and Bailey's line of waiting customers grew to eight. Somehow, she crammed down two hot dogs and drank a sixteen-ounce soda without slowing down.

The afternoon began with Deputy Salinski ambling around the booth. Fen noticed he paid little attention to the paintings and seemed to be waiting for an opening to talk. After a customer failed to bargain down the price of a painting depicting a crop of winter wheat ravaged by hail, Fen gave the deputy his attention.

"Hello, Ski. I wanted to thank you for turning on your camera the day I came to the office."

"I would say no problem, but Lieutenant Creech put me on nights after he found out."

"That may be a blessing in disguise. Sometimes it's best to keep a low profile."

Ski responded with an unconvincing, "Yeah. I guess you're right."

The lackluster words caused Fen to suspect something else was on Ski's mind. "I didn't have you pegged as an art lover."

"Guilty. I wanted to let you know I'm not sure how much longer I can hold out with my current employer, and ask if you had any recommendations about where I should apply."

"Is it that bad?"

The bill of his baseball cap came down and back up in sharp movements. "Drugs are taking over the county and it's open season on us who want to do something about it."

Fen took in enough air to make the material on his shirt

pucker where the buttons joined it together. "If you want to stay local, you might try the city police department."

"They're at full strength with three former deputies already hoping to get on. There's no position open for constables, either."

"What about DPS? You'd make a good State Trooper."

"Not enough education."

Fen nodded. "That would probably keep you from most federal jobs, too. If you want to stay in law enforcement, your best bet would be to try a department somewhere other than this county."

"I was afraid you'd say that. Any other ideas?"

"There's always the state prison system. With all the units spread around the state, they might assign you to one near here. It's not law enforcement, but they're under the same retirement plan as DPS. You should be able to get promoted pretty fast."

Ski tilted his hat farther back on his head. "Gina and I had everything planned to live out our lives here around family. Maybe things will change at the sheriff's department. I'll try to stick it out as long as I can." He tilted his head. "What I'd give to have you back running things."

"Thanks, but my days as sheriff are over. Hang in there. Something tells me changes are coming."

The two shook hands and Fen moved on to a customer with a magnifying glass, examining a scene of deer and feral hogs browsing in a field of oats. When Fen finished with this non-buyer, he spotted Trudy Greenwood speaking with Bailey as she sketched. Both bore smiles as the student artist showed her teacher a pile of money in a plastic container.

Trudy handed out a hug and made her way to Fen. He touched the bill of his hat and issued a formal, "Good afternoon, Miss Greenwood. Your prized student is doing well for herself."

She flapped her arms like a penguin. “If I was any happier, I’d split right down the middle. Not only are you here, but you’ve taken Bailey under your wing. The word’s out about how you saved her from jail this morning. If I could reach high enough, I’d give you a kiss that would get all kinds of rumors started.”

Fen couldn’t help but chuckle. “If we’re going to start rumors, let’s do it right. Candy Forsythe told me to take Bailey out for a nice dinner tonight. How would you like to join us?”

Trudy slapped both hands over her mouth to stifle a squeal of delight. When she controlled herself, she asked, “Does Bailey know?”

“She’s been so swamped today I didn’t want to interrupt her. Why don’t you tell her?”

“Where are we going?”

“Wherever you want.”

“Let’s go to Casa del Mar. I know she likes Tex-Mex.”

Fen gave his head a firm nod. “Deal.” He ran his hand across his chin. “The festival is over at five-thirty. It will take me about forty-five minutes to pack and another fifteen to get to the restaurant. Can you meet us there around six thirty?”

“Many hands make light work, and I have nothing to do for the rest of the day. I’ll stick around and help you load your truck. That way, Bailey can ride with me to the restaurant and I’ll take her home. Let’s not give people too much to talk about.”

A handshake sealed the conversation. When Bailey heard the plan, she turned enough to respond with a smile and a nod. It lasted only a second or two, but Fen’s chest tightened. It had been so long since he felt joy that it scared him.

It wasn’t until late afternoon that the crowds thinned. That’s when County Judge Rawlings and Justice of the Peace Harley Stone walked into the booth. Handshakes were exchanged. Harley moved away to look at paintings, as Judge

Rawlings stayed by Fen's side and pointed at an evening scene where low, black clouds from a blue norther rolled ominously across the stubble left from a harvest. A lone steer stood in the foreground, looking at nature displaying impending doom.

"This scene speaks of bad times."

Fen remembered when he painted it and silently agreed. "Someone once said that for every laugh there has to be a tear."

"I'm not sure about the proportion of tears to laughter, but there's a lot of truth in that statement. It's also true that good and bad times come and go like seasons. The important thing is to not give up hope that a new season is coming." He took a step back from the work on display. "Take this painting, for instance. If I was a rancher standing in that field, I'd be running for cover. There's nothing that cuts through you like being caught out in a driving rain and a forty-degree drop in temperature. Whatever I was doing would come to a halt, and I'd find a snug living room with a roaring fire."

Fen nodded. The judge captured in words what he hoped to say through the painting.

Judge Rawlings acknowledged Fen's nod and kept talking. "What I don't see in this painting is what the rancher will do if he needs to get that steer out of the way of the storm. Are there other cattle? If so, does he move them to higher ground in case the river floods? Does he put out extra hay and make sure they have water? What about predators? He may have to leave his cozy living room and take care of that lone steer, or an entire herd."

After clearing his throat, Fen turned to face the Judge. "I think I know what you're trying to say, but lightning struck the rancher, and he's not recovered enough to be any good to anyone."

The judge's lip quirked. "Seasons come and go. By looking at this painting, I bet the rancher already knows about the threats to the herd." He turned, looked at Bailey, and then back again to Fen. "I'd like to commission a painting of the rancher saving a stray calf. If it turns out the way I hope it will, I may order another of him tending his herd."

Fen turned to the gray-haired judge with wise eyes. "I'll start sketching the calf in the morning. I can't commit to the second painting."

Hands joined in agreement as Fen wondered what he'd gotten himself into. He had little time to think about it. As soon as Judge Rawlings and Harley Stone left, the man with the magnifying glass returned and purchased the painting he'd so thoroughly examined. It was Fen's last sale of the day, but it put the cap on his most successful day ever. It was a good thing. Bailey had kept scrupulous records on the number of students' and children's sketches she'd done and presented Fen with his bill as soon as an air horn blew to end the festival.

"You did an acceptable job today," said Fen. "I suppose you want cash instead of a check."

"Cash works for me," said Bailey as she shifted from one foot to the other. "I'll be right back." She took off at a run.

Fen looked at Trudy. "What's gotten into her?"

"Sixteen ounces of Coke and a bottle of water. She didn't get out of that chair all day."

He wanted to slap his forehead. He'd definitely been away from people too long. "I'll start packing. I don't know about you, but I may order two entrees."

Chapter Eleven

The trio of Fen, Bailey, and Trudy Greenwood had to wait ten minutes to be seated. The hostess announced Fen's name, gathered menus, and led them through a maze of tables to a back room that was normally closed off. It seemed as if half the town wanted to end their day at the festival with a substantial meal. Along the way, Fen nodded greetings to several who addressed him as Sheriff Maguire.

Once seated, Bailey asked, "Is there anyone in the place that doesn't know you?"

Fen couldn't help but smile. "That's what happens when you're elected to a public office like sheriff."

"Why aren't you the sheriff now?"

Fen stiffened when he saw Lori Newman, her father Nathaniel, and Jake Creech walking toward them. Mr. Newman spotted him as they drew near the empty table next to theirs and gave him a frozen rope stare. Out of the corner of his eye, Fen noticed Bailey tense as Lieutenant Creech approached. He wasn't in uniform, but she'd spotted him all the same.

"This table won't do," said Fen's former father-in-law. "I'll not sit in the same room as a criminal."

It wasn't until he lodged his complaint that Lori looked at Fen and spoke loud enough to draw the gaze of other patrons. "Like my father said, this is unacceptable. I made reservations for six o'clock in the main dining room."

The hostess dry washed her hands. "Yes, ma'am. We held a table open for you until six thirty. If you want to wait for another table, or a booth, I'll be happy to put you on the list."

Mr. Newman glared at Fen but addressed his words to the server. "Never mind. We'll take our business elsewhere."

Lori added. "Tell the manager to expect a phone call from Sheriff Newman."

Not to be left out, Creech took a step toward Fen, held up three fingers, and gave a malevolent smile. He spun on the soles of new boots and followed father and daughter.

"What was that all about?" asked Bailey in a voice that should have been more discreet.

"Long story," said Fen as he rose. "I'm going to wash my hands."

Once in the restroom, he splashed water on his face. The day had been the best of the year except for the last five minutes. He told himself to buck up and not allow his past to ruin Bailey's successful day.

"We ordered you iced tea," said Trudy as Fen took his seat. "It may not be as good as you get at home, but it should wet your whistle."

"As thirsty as I am, I'd drink muddy water out of the river."

"Yuk," said Bailey as she attacked another tortilla chip dipped in salsa. "Of course, the water out of the tap isn't much better. One thing I'm spending my money on is two or three cases of Dr. Pepper."

Trudy leaned forward. "What else will you buy?"

Bailey wrapped a lock of hair around her index finger. "The usual things: food and some different clothes at a thrift store. Of course, I'll need to pay the water and electric bills." She took the cover off a straw. "Oh yeah. Also, a couple of fans would be nice. That trailer is like an oven."

"Why would you need a fan with winter coming on?"

"The air conditioning went out the day after I moved here at the end of August. I promised myself I'd buy a fan as soon as I got the money."

Fen asked, "Is it just you and your mom in Uncle Clete's house now?"

Bailey dipped her head as she answered, "Yeah." She looked up. "I want to talk to you about Uncle Clete."

The discussion had to wait as the server came to take orders. Fen was the last in line and ordered fajitas for two.

While Bailey continued to scarf down triangular tortilla chips, Fen wanted to hear what she had to say about Clete. "Now's as good a time as any. Let's talk about your uncle."

Bailey put down a chip and leaned toward him. "I want to hire you to find the person who killed him."

Trudy reacted before Fen could. "That's what the police do, and Mr. Fen is no longer the sheriff."

"So? From what I've seen of the cops around here, they're too busy making money on the side to mess with the murder of an old druggie like my uncle."

Fen tilted his head and lowered his voice. "What do you mean, they're making money on the side?"

Bailey lowered her voice and checked around before saying, "Do you know the woods on the property next to the mobile home I'm living in?"

Fen nodded. "That property belongs to Mr. Newman, the new sheriff's father."

Bailey looked in the direction Mr. Newman had left the room. "That old man doesn't look the type."

"What type would that be?"

Bailey leaned on the table with both arms. "There's an opening in the woods on that property that's covered with an army surplus camo net. It lets in plenty of sunshine to grow plants with jagged leaves. Uncle Clete called it his cash crop. I followed him without his knowing and watched him harvest some of his crop. I've also seen sheriff's department vehicles block off both ends of the road at night while someone driving a black pickup comes and picks up large full plastic bags."

Fen leaned back. "It doesn't surprise me that Clete had a cottage business going, but I'm having a hard time believing Lori's father knows that's happening on his land."

It was Trudy's turn to lean forward. "The growing of pot doesn't concern me as much as what's going on in school. I'm hearing more and more reports of students using hard drugs."

Bailey dipped another chip into salsa. "This school isn't much different from what I went to in Houston. If you have the money, you can get anything you want."

Fen looked at both of them. "You're both looking at me like I should do something about it. In case you missed the last election results, I'm not the sheriff. I have no authority to investigate crimes of any kind."

"So what?" asked Bailey. "Get a badge of some sort and say you're a private investigator. I bet you can still carry a gun in this state. Heck, almost everyone else in Texas packs heat."

Fen shook his head. "I'll pass on the information you both gave me to people I know and trust. As for tonight, let's relax and enjoy the feast that's coming our way."

Halfway through the meal, Fen looked at Bailey. "You're living by yourself in Uncle Clete's trailer, aren't you?"

Trudy gasped.

Bailey stopped chewing and squared her shoulders. Her chin lifted in defiance. "Mom tries to come on weekends."

"When is your birthday?"

"On Halloween I'll be eighteen."

Fen looked at Trudy. "Child Protective Services wouldn't have time to process her. I don't know about you, but I heard nothing about her living alone."

Trudy looked at Fen and then at Bailey. "I was crunching on a taco and missed what you two said."

With fork in hand, Fen pointed to what remained of the mound of charred meat, singed onions and bell peppers, guacamole, *pico de gallo,* and flour tortillas in the center of the table. "You two help yourselves. I'm stuffed."

Trudy pushed her plate a few inches toward the center of the table. "I'll have to waddle out of here as it is."

Bailey looked at the mounds of food remaining. "I wish I could, but I ate too many chips. Can I get a to-go box?"

"Sure." He paused. "There's something else I want to ask you, Bailey."

She tilted her head and asked, "What?"

"I'm coming up on the busy time of year for selling art. There's a big Halloween carnival two counties over to the west in a couple of weeks. It's like what we did today, only bigger. Would you be interested in earning some more money?"

"Heck, yeah, if it's the same deal."

"Same deal. Then we get into Thanksgiving and the Christmas celebrations. That's six weekends straight of places to go. I'll probably run out of paintings, but we could both do caricatures."

Her face shone with excitement. "I could work on paintings after school and bring them if you run out." She paused. "Wait. That won't work. I don't have the supplies I'll need."

Trudy's eyes brightened. "I have enough money in the

budget to get you brushes and I have a canvas or two of my own I can give you."

Fen said, "I'll front you the money for everything else you'll need, but I have a reputation to uphold. I want your paintings to be first rate, and in acrylic."

"Why not oil?"

"Have you ever painted with oils?"

"Once. It smeared all over the place."

"That's because it takes so long to dry. Also, oil paints are too expensive to waste."

Bailey bristled. "I wouldn't waste them."

Trudy reached over and touched Bailey's hand. "You have talent, but it takes years of practice to become proficient in oils. Listen to what Mr. Fen is telling you."

Bailey spoke with confidence. "I'll have plenty of money to buy oils and anything else if I work six or seven more fairs."

Fen ignored her and looked at Trudy for help, but nothing came except a wide grin and sparkling eyes.

Something occurred to Fen. "What will you do with your money if you make five, ten, fifteen thousand dollars, or more?"

Bailey's eyes darted back and forth. "I'll buy a car... or a truck like yours so I could keep doing fairs."

"Good answer. What do you need to make that happen?"

She shrugged in a way that said she didn't know.

"You need a new driver's license. Take care of that tonight."

"Can't."

"Why not?"

"No Internet at the trailer."

Trudy came to the rescue again. "I have my laptop in my car. We'll go to the Shake Shack, get an ice cream cone, and log on there. Then I'll take you home."

The server arrived with the check and a to-go box without being asked. She winked at Bailey. "I saw the drawing you did for my cousin. You're as good as Sheriff Maguire." She placed a hand on his shoulder. "Almost as good."

Fen paid the bill and met Bailey outside the front door. "Where's Trudy? Er, Miss Greenwood?"

Bailey looked up at him. "She's bringing her car around to pick me up. I told her I needed a minute with you alone."

"Yes?"

Bailey looked up at him with questioning eyes. "What's the catch? You didn't have to do anything for me today."

"It's complicated," said Fen.

"I'm smarter than you think I am. I'll figure you out."

"I'm just an honest farmer trying to get by."

"You can sell that load of hay to someone else. And one more thing, I'm not giving up on you. You're the one who'll find Uncle Clete's killer."

On the way home, Fen mulled over Bailey's suggestion that he become a private investigator. He'd dismissed the idea by the time he punched in the code to his front gate.

Chapter Twelve

Fen sipped a glass of iced tea and reviewed what he'd accomplished the week after the harvest festival. Sketches of the calf came easy, but not so much for the rancher that would rescue the newborn. It occurred to him that Judge Rawlings hadn't mentioned a price for the work. He shrugged off the oversight. The judge was up to date with current market values of the two paintings he'd previously bought, and he was honest to the point of being overly generous. It didn't hurt that the land that Judge Rawlings inherited bristled with oil pumps and storage tanks. A slice of Fen's property had several wells too, but not as many as Judge Rawlings or Fen's former father-in-law.

Out of curiosity, Fen spent an evening exploring the Internet, studying qualifications to become a licensed private investigator. His law enforcement certification hadn't expired, but it would if he wasn't working for an agency or department. He mouthed a near silent, "Oh, why not?" and filled out an application.

While online, he placed a substantial order for canvases,

paints, sketch pads, and artist's pencils with leads of various degrees of hardness. He thought of Bailey and her lack of nuance in shading that came from using a soft-lead pencil and rubbing to form shadows.

He also called Highway Patrol Sergeant Tom Stevens and informed him of the camouflaged pot garden on Nathaniel Newman's land. He recalled the conversation.

"Doesn't surprise me," said Tom. "Nathaniel Newman owns so much land in this county, he probably never checks those woods. How big is the plot?"

"It can't be too big if they have it covered with a camo net."

"Not much of a crime. Something the county should handle. Besides, I'm sitting in a lawn chair at Port Aransas, hoping a fish doesn't strike my bait. I'll be here for the next five days. Who do you know at the sheriff's department that we can trust to look into it?"

"Salinski would be my choice. I know he's looking to leave if things don't improve."

"I heard a rumor Ski put in an application with the prison system. I'll call him and see if he'll check it out." He paused and chuckled. "I take it you want to remain as an anonymous informant?"

"You're too good at reading my mind. You'll make a fine sheriff someday."

Fen came back to the present and made a faint mark on his canvas to establish a horizon line. The colors would reflect sunshine with broken clouds to give hints of shadows. It would be a scene that captured a cowboy, his horse, and a mud-covered calf being carried away from a rain-swollen creek leading to the river. Details in the composition eluded him, but he knew they would come with time. The past year had shown him time was a commodity he had in abundance.

A knock on the door of his studio brought his gaze from the canvas and he hollered, "Come in, Thelma."

She opened the door but didn't enter his sanctum. "That gal called this morning while you were having your time with Miss Sally."

"Her name is Bailey. What did she want?"

"Said she needs two more canvases and some tubes of paint."

"What colors?"

"She talked so fast my ears couldn't keep up. That child must have studied speed-speaking in school."

"Can she out-talk you?"

Thelma let out a cackle. "She's good, but she ain't that good."

"I'll have Sam run the supplies by her place this afternoon. He's going to the feed store, and it will save me a trip."

"I know where that man goes and what he does. You don't have to tell me."

It never ceased to amaze him how the most unlikely husband and wife he'd ever met kept up with each other. One of the great mysteries of Newman County.

Fen laid down his brush and looked out the window. The late October sun was giving way to darkness. The grumble of his stomach reminded him he'd skipped lunch. He'd finished washing his brushes when Thelma banged on the door. Instead of waiting for permission to enter, she barged in. "Mr. Fen. That man of mine is on his way home and he's mad as a cowboy whose horse ran off and left him to walk."

"What happened?"

"Something about him getting pulled over by a sheriff's

deputy. He was jabbering in that other language so much I couldn't understand him."

Fen stretched. It was out of character for Sam to express anger, but he'd seen it once or twice before. "I'll talk to Sam about it when he gets home." He moved toward the door. "I hope you fixed a big supper."

"Same portions as usual. If you're still hungry, you can eat the sandwich I made for you at noon. Call it a new dessert if you like."

Despite his growling stomach, Fen told Thelma he'd hold off on supper until Sam returned. He pondered what traffic violation Sam might have committed. His foreman prided himself on keeping all the vehicles on the farm in top working order and it was out of character for Sam to speed. In fact, he did most everything at a calm, even, steady pace.

When the pickup pulled into the circular driveway, Fen was there. "I heard you had a little trouble."

Sam mumbled something in Choctaw. He then crooked his finger and motioned for Fen to follow him to the back of the truck. It took only a glance for Fen to see the broken plastic on the driver's side taillight.

"A deputy sheriff?" asked Fen.

Sam nodded.

"He used his flashlight?"

Another nod.

Fen heaved a sigh. "I'll take care of the ticket."

Sam handed it to him.

"Two can play this game. I'll order tiny cameras with microphones for all the vehicles. You'll need to mount them in places a cop wouldn't expect. Make sure they don't stand out. If this happens again, keep your cool and don't give them an excuse to arrest you." Fen tilted his head. "What did you say to him?"

"Nothing bad in English."

"What about in Choctaw?"

"It doesn't translate well. I compared the deputy's face with the sweaty rump of a buffalo with its tail up."

Fen maintained a straight face by looking away. He cleared his throat. "Did you deliver the paint supplies to Bailey?"

Sam nodded. "She lives in a dump. The roof leaks and there's mold."

"That's why she never let me come in." Fen turned back to Sam. "I'm working on something better for her, but I can't do it yet."

Sam opened the door to his truck and climbed in. "Tell Thelma to let me know when the cameras arrive. I'll be somewhere on the property until they do."

THE PHONE CALL came at first light, three days before Halloween. Fen was on his first mug of coffee, sitting in his study to have his morning talk with Sally when his phone rang. He looked at the name on the screen and punched the icon to speak with Tom Stevens.

"This can't be good news."

"It's not. I'm working a near-fatality on County Road 416 where it makes a ninety-degree turn at Sam Reynolds' pecan orchard."

Fen closed his eyes. "Keep talking."

"It's Ski."

A moan escaped Fen's lips as Tom continued. "He was in pursuit of a black truck. It appears he lost control on the curve, fishtailed twice, went through a barbed-wire fence, and slammed into a pecan tree with the driver's side door."

Fen pictured the wreck and had questions. "Did they catch the driver of the black truck?"

"Nope."

"How long had Ski been in pursuit?"

"Three minutes."

Fen rubbed his chin. "That should have been enough time for other deputies to respond and get a visual."

"He was the only one on that side of the county."

"That's not right. I never allowed deputies to congregate like that."

"That young deputy with the bad complexion told me Ski should have been on patrol way to the east. They bunched all the other deputies up on that side of the county. I'm thinking Ski was following up on the lead you gave me."

"How serious are the injuries?"

"Bad enough for them to med-evac him to Austin."

With cheeks puffed out, Fen released a full breath as Tom continued. "It looks like he lost control, but I have a hunch there's more to the story."

"Me too. Ski knew every inch of the roads on that side of the county."

"I spoke with Sheriff Lori and told her she needed to call in Danni Worth to do a crime scene investigation. She's taking this hard."

"Which 'she' are you talking about? Lori or Danni?"

"Sheriff Lori's fighting back tears. Danni's mad as a wet cat. She told me she'll do what she can, but wants to have a better look at Ski's vehicle at the impound yard."

A few seconds of silence passed before Fen spoke. "The real reason you called was to ask me if I'd had enough of what's going on in the county. Am I right?"

"I talked to my lieutenant and captain. They told me

there's not enough for them to call in the Rangers to investigate. I'm not to get involved in local politics."

Fen paused long enough to let out a full breath of exasperation. "I'll talk to Chuck Forsythe and tell him I'm looking into a few things. There's a good chance Lieutenant Creech will get his wish and arrest me."

"Do you want to communicate with me directly or through Chuck?"

"Let's go through Chuck, unless it's an emergency. There needs to be a legal firewall between me and you. Attorney/client confidentiality should protect both of us." He paused. "By the way, I've applied for a PI license. It's not worth much, but it gives me an excuse to ask questions."

"Who's your client?"

"That's confidential. If Chuck thinks you need to know, he'll tell you."

Chapter Thirteen

Fen picked up a copy of the bi-weekly newspaper as he entered the Black Gold Cafe. The name could have referred to the substantial oil deposits in the county or the color and texture of the coffee served. Some loved the extra-strong brew while others likened it to sludge. The biscuits, however, were in a league of their own. The fluffy treasures measured five inches by five inches at the base and rose to a height of three and a half inches. A bowl of sausage gravy accompanied every two-biscuit order, which more than made up for any shortcomings with the coffee.

Fen requested the lone booth in a back corner. A homemade cardboard sign reading RESERVED topped the oval-shaped table for eight next to where he sat. He ordered coffee and a half order of biscuits and gravy. Not long after he took his first sip a gathering of elderly gentlemen assembled around the table. Known to townsfolk as the spit-and-whittle coffee clutch, none whittled or spit, at least not in the diner, but they met daily at Black Gold to give their opinion on all things related to politics, economics, and current events.

An hour and fifteen minutes later, Fen was up-to-date on the topic du jour. Specifically, Salinski's pursuit and near-fatal injuries. After exhausting the pursuit and crash with as much speculation as facts, the spit-and-whittles moved on to discuss the state of the sheriff's office. Opinions of the new sheriff ranged from low to a desire for a recall election. It was as Fen expected.

Candy looked up as he arrived at Chuck Forsythe's law office a little before eight-thirty. He knew Chuck eased into Fridays by reading the local paper. Candy walked him to Chuck's office and found the attorney with boots on his desk and the newspaper spread across his lap.

Chuck looked over the glasses perched on his nose. "I was wondering what it would take to draw you out of your cave. Have you read today's edition?"

Fen took a seat on the client side of Chuck's desk. "It's worse than what you're reading. The spit-and-whittles want to send Lori packing, and I've applied for a private investigator's license."

Chuck's mouth hinged open. "I wasn't expecting the second one." He lowered his feet and tapped his fingers on the desk. "Now that I think about it, why not? This keeps you out of law enforcement but gives you an excuse to stick your nose into Lori's business. I like it."

"You approve because you know I'll probably wind up in jail, and you'll have to come rescue me."

A grin parted Chuck's lips. "It isn't often this job is fun, but I have a feeling that things may get downright hilarious. Tell me what your primary concerns are."

"Did you read the entire article?"

Chuck nodded. "The reporter that moved from Dallas wrote it. Someone fed the story to her."

Fen opened his newspaper to the front page. "I'll skip the part about Salinski's chase and injuries."

> *"According to reliable sources, the sheriff's office knew Mr. Nathaniel Newman owned the land where the police chase began and that Deputy Salinski was investigating the illegal drug operation on his own. It's further alleged that Sheriff Lori Newman knew her father was profiting from this illegal activity.*
> *The same source said that a copy of a forensic report from the Texas Department of Public Safety shows a pistol belonging to Sheriff Newman is, in fact, the gun used to murder Mr. Cletus Brumbaugh. Sheriff Newman and her father refused to deny allegations or give a statement."*

Fen then flipped over several pages. "Did you read the editorial?"

Chuck barely moved his head up and down before he said, "Marge didn't cut Lori or her father any slack. She had a lot more dirt on the sheriff's office than I was aware of. If it's all true, Lori might not last long as sheriff."

Fen folded the newspaper and placed it on the corner of Chuck's desk. "I told Tom Stevens I'd turn over what I found to him and you'd be our go-between."

An even larger grin came from the attorney. "I like it so much I'll take credit for thinking of it first." He tilted his head. "How long have you been sitting back, waiting for the right moment to get on the hunt?"

"I've had my eyes and ears open ever since Clete floated past me on the river."

"Should have known. Candy said you wouldn't sit this one out."

Fen took three steps toward the door, stopped, and turned. "I almost forgot. Sam received this from one of the new deputies." He handed Chuck the citation for the broken taillight.

Chuck scanned it and fixed his gaze on one particular line. "The old broken tail light scam?"

"Yep."

"That means someone's after you and they're not above going after someone who's loyal to you." He threw the ticket on his desk. "Don't worry about it. I'll contest it and have Lena at the J.P.'s office schedule the deputy to show up on his day off. Then, I'll get a postponement. Two or three times of doing that and the deputy won't show up to testify."

Fen shook his head. "You know that's not how I roll."

Chuck let out a huff. "Oh, all right. I'll find another way, and I won't tell you what it is. By the way, how long before I have to bail you out of jail?"

"It may not be long. I'm going to talk to Lori. This evening I'm checking on Bailey before we leave for the Halloween carnival tomorrow. I'm hoping we'll do as well as we did at the Harvest Festival. While I'm there, I'll search Clete's trailer; if I'm lucky, the deputies missed something important."

Chuck raised his mug in a toast. "I'll drink to that."

Once in his truck, Fen called Brenda on her cell phone. The dispatcher answered in a whisper, "Sheriff Maguire?"

"Yeah, Brenda. It's me, and I need you to do me a favor."

"Name it."

"Leave the door to the offices ajar. I need to talk to Lori and if I try to get past her new gatekeepers, they won't let me see her."

"How long before you're here?"

"Two minutes."

"That door's been sticking. It wouldn't surprise me if it's been open all morning."

"Thanks. I owe you."

"You can repay me by being sheriff again."

Not only did Brenda leave the door ajar, she had the deputy controlling access to the offices and holding cells involved in a conversation. Brenda ranted on about how concerned she was about Salinski, his wife, and the baby. Fen slipped through the door on the balls of his feet, making sure the heels of his boots didn't give his presence away.

He walked down the hall to his former office, turned the knob, and strode in like he was still sheriff. He had the door shut behind him before Lori raised her head from a stack of papers. Her surprise delayed a response and gave him time to slide into a chair in front of her desk. He hooked his left boot over his right knee. "I need to talk to you, Lori. Somebody's trying to set you up."

"How did you get in here?"

"The door to the hallway was open. That remote access button never worked right, but that's not important. What's important is—"

She cut him off with a sharp, "Get out!"

"You need to listen to me. Someone's trying to destroy your father's reputation and drive you out of office."

Her eyebrows drew together and a color he'd describe as sunset-pink crept up her neck. "Do you think I'm so stupid that I haven't figured that out yet?" A finger pointed at him. "And I'm looking at the man who'd do anything to get his old job back." She rose from her seat. "You took a year off from the Harvest Festival pretending to mourn my sister." She stood straight as a new fence post. "You might have mourned for a while, but not a full year. You used that time to paint your stupid pictures and plot how you could drive me out. I never thought you'd be so low as to go after my father. When did you and that cute reporter from Dallas hook up? Hmm?"

Fen shook his head in denial. "Who's been feeding you those lies?"

The blood continued to travel upward, into her face. "Don't talk to me about lies. I haven't gotten rid of all the liars in this department yet, but it won't be much longer."

Fen remained seated and calm. "Like Salinski? He wasn't where your boy Creech thought he would be. He was doing actual work, not trying to find excuses to run off good men and women."

Lori tented her hands on her hips. "It's Salinski's fault for forgetting who's the new sheriff. He's in the hospital because he wasn't on patrol where he should have been."

Fen shook his head and stood. "He's clinging to life because you don't know a patrol pattern from a dress pattern. Check where all the deputies were when Ski started the pursuit. Ask yourself why your boy Creech had every deputy on duty so far east they couldn't come to assist."

Lori moved to the door and opened it, only to see Lt. Creech jogging toward her.

"What's wrong Lori? I heard loud voices."

Fen moved to the door, invaded Creech's space and gave him a glare he'd perfected on uncooperative teens. "I said what I came to say, and I'm leaving."

Creech looked past Fen to Lori. "What did he say to you?"

"It was mainly about a family matter," said Fen. "And it's none of your business."

Creech took two steps back and placed his hand where his gun should have been.

Fen shook his head to mock the lieutenant for wanting to draw his weapon. "I designed these offices to have access to the booking area in case officers needed help. No weapons allowed on this side of the control gate."

"I don't need a gun to arrest you."

"What for? Talking with my wife's sister?"

"Being in an unauthorized area."

"The door was open. Isn't security of this building one of your responsibilities? I'm sure the newspaper has plenty of paper and ink for another story with your name and photo on the front page."

Lori shouted, "Get out, and don't come back!"

Fen turned and gave her a look that combined resolve with pity. "Watch your back, Lori. We never had a problem with snakes in this building, but you have an infestation that's only getting worse."

The drive home gave Fen a chance to think and wonder if his visit had done more harm than good. He pulled off the road and parked in the shade of the bridge over the Brazos. He took out his cell phone and called Chuck.

"Did they arrest you?"

"Not yet, but I stirred up a mound of fire ants. Do you want details?"

"Send me an email. I'll relay what you've done to Tom Stevens." He paused. "I have to go. Good luck with the search of Clete's trailer and have fun at the Halloween carnival tomorrow."

Time had no meaning as Fen watched the river as it flowed by at a slow, steady pace. The surface looked like a long, winding length of brown ribbon. In most places it was shiny-smooth, but in the places with ripples the river gave away its secrets of hidden obstacles and unseen currents. He concluded a person can learn a lot from staring at the Brazos.

Chapter Fourteen

At first glance from the road, the single-wide trailer that had been Clete Brumbaugh's home looked tired and in need of serious upkeep. Fen considered calling a tow truck to remove a couple of rusting cars without wheels in the yard, but decided against it until he spoke with Bailey. As he stepped closer to the small, sagging front porch, the more convinced he was that the trailer was likely unfit for human occupancy. Overlooking the porch were two windows, their glass replaced with plywood held in place with gray duct tape. Streaks of green and brown ran from the roof.

He looked at his watch to make sure it was past time for the school bus to have delivered Bailey, knocked on the front door, and waited for a reply that didn't come. Served him right for not calling. He took his chances with what creatures might lurk inside and tried the front door. It was unlocked, so he went in, put on gloves and found what he believed to be Clete's bedroom. He wasn't sure if the former occupant was in competition for the slovenly man award, or if an indoor cyclone had struck the room.

A call from the front yard interrupted his search. He made it to the door to see Bailey dismount a boy's bicycle and let it fall among other pieces of Clete's discarded life. "Fen? What are you doing here?"

He pointed to the bicycle. "Where'd you get the wheels?"

"I bought it at a yard sale. Do you have any idea how embarrassing it is for an eighteen-year-old senior to get on a yellow school bus every day?"

"You're not eighteen until tomorrow. Is that how you get around these days?"

"It's better than walking."

"We're at least four miles outside of town and it's another two to the high school."

She looked at him with hands on her hips. "Duh. Tell me something I don't know." She cocked her head. "What are you doing here?"

He responded with a question of his own. "Why are you so late getting home?"

She flipped her ponytail. "You sound like my mom. To answer your question, I stopped at the Shake Shack to eat supper."

He looked down. "Celebrating your birthday a day early?"

Bailey walked past him into the living room, took off her backpack and let it fall on a couch with a brick under one corner where a wooden leg should have been. "You're not much of a detective, are you?"

"What do you mean?"

"You've been snooping around and you didn't realize the refrigerator isn't working and I'm out of propane."

He looked at her and slowed the pace of his questions. "Rough day at school?"

She responded by saying, "I'm not going back." She didn't

give him time to respond before she said, "I thought you weren't coming until tomorrow morning."

Fen thought about challenging her on the statement about leaving high school, but left that issue for another day. Instead, he focused on his real reason for coming. "I was looking at Clete's bedroom. What happened?"

"That lieutenant that wears his shirts tight to show off his muscles and some blond lady tore the trailer apart right after they fished Uncle Clete out of the river."

"Lieutenant Creech?"

"The one and only. At school, we call him Lieutenant Creep." She held a hand out toward Clete's bedroom. "They started in there and worked their way through the entire trailer. I had to wait outside while they did their best to destroy everything they could."

"Who was the woman?"

"Beats me. A few years younger than you. Tight jeans, curvy, someone broke her nose a long time ago."

Fen nodded. "That's Danni Worth, the crime scene investigator. It makes sense that she'd be looking for clues. She's normally not destructive when she processes a room. Did she do that to Clete's room?"

"Didn't you hear me? They made me wait outside."

"Front or back?"

"On the back porch."

Bailey gave a quick tilt to her head toward the back door. "Come see the paintings I'm taking in the morning."

Fen followed her to a screened-in room built onto the back of the trailer. He noted a fold-up rollaway bed in one corner and a large fan on a stand. It was, by far, the most pleasant place to live on the property. A cedar tree along one side of the porch and two pots of rosemary by the screen door leading to the yard gave off scents that complemented the crisp smell of being outdoors as the season changed to fall.

He scanned the backyard. Fifty yards of grass bowed its head, following an early frost several days ago. An abandoned wooden outhouse stood where thick grass met a stand of trees and bushes. "Nice spot. Looks like you sleep out here."

"For now. Until it gets too cold. It's been pretty nice since I got the fan."

"Is this where you do all your painting?"

Bailey moved to a stack of canvases propped up against the trailer. "The light out here isn't bad on the weekends, but I have to use a lamp and run an extension cord from inside at night. Blending colors to match doesn't work well when I switch from natural light to a bulb."

Fen nodded in agreement and examined her works one-by-one. He put the last one down and gave his appraisal. "I can tell which ones you painted this week. You rushed them."

"So? They're the best I could do with the time I had."

He shook his head. "Your name is the most important thing you'll have in the world of art. I'd rather see you sell one painting for five hundred dollars than ten at a hundred dollars each."

"But I'd make twice as much money."

"And you'll be trying to sell paintings for a hundred dollars for the rest of your life." He looked down at her small face. "Trust me. Leave the paintings that you know are inferior and only take the ones you know are good."

Muscles worked in her jaw. "I painted until 2:00 a.m. for weeks working on those. I'm selling them tomorrow."

"I sell quality art, not something someone slapped together." Fen shook his head and pointed to the stack. "I'll not allow you to ruin your reputation by peddling works that don't show your talent."

"My reputation?" Bailey put fire in her stare. "In case you haven't noticed, the only reputation I have is as a loser from Houston. You can paint when you want, but I am not a rich cattle baron. I ride a second-hand bicycle and wear other people's discarded clothes. I steal when I have to. All I have is my ability to draw and put paint on canvas."

Fen took in a full breath and stared back. "I didn't always have money. I'll admit that you had it rougher growing up than I did. Congratulations, you win that blue ribbon for having a lousy childhood." His words came faster. "But I worked my way through college selling sketches and caricatures. I refused to sell paintings that didn't measure up to my standards. I also listened to people who knew what makes a painting worthy of people shelling out their hard-earned money. Quality takes time and you haven't put in enough."

Her chin quivered. He sensed his resolve fading, but steeled himself. "We're leaving at five in the morning. You're taking four paintings. That's all. I'm going to do my best to sell them. While I'm doing that, you'll be smiling at people you don't know and making money by exaggerating people's body parts. Questions?"

Bailey's chin stopped quivering, which confirmed his belief that she used this trick to get her way. Her words came out rough. "Yeah. When are you going to look for who killed Uncle Clete, and why do some people say you allowed your wife to die when you could have saved her?"

A shiver went down Fen's spine as his fingernails dug into his palms. Every muscle tightened. He allowed his stare into Bailey's defiant eyes to have its full effect and finally spoke in a harsh whisper. "Never ask me about Sally again."

The small porch was suddenly closing in. Fen had to get outside. He tried to spin on the rough-cut boards of the porch, but the heel of his boot caught. His unstable knee played an early Halloween trick on him and he fell. A searing pain shot from his knee to his brain, causing him to cry out.

Bailey was at his side in a flash, the defiance in her eyes replaced with concern. Was it because of his pain or was she seeing her chances of earning much needed money disappear? Either way, he was glad there was someone to help.

"Let me rest a few minutes before I try to get up."

She retrieved a dining room chair with a metal frame and a padded seat from inside the trailer. "When you're ready, I'll help you."

"You're going to have to do more than that."

"What do you mean?"

"I came here to look for clues. If you're up to it, you'll help me go from room to room with this chair. I'll tell you where to look."

Bailey's eyes widened. "You're looking for Uncle Clete's killer?"

"That's why I'm here. Unless you want to keep arguing, we'll go inside and search for something the others missed."

"You won't find anything. I already looked. Why don't we put this off until Sunday? You need to ice that knee or you'll be useless tomorrow."

Fen took his time considering her words. On the one hand, the trailer wasn't going anywhere and two searches had already taken place, the first by two professionals. It seemed Bailey's motives for the delay might be selfish. He needed to test her.

"We'll delay the search until Sunday afternoon, and you're still taking only the four paintings I choose."

Bailey pinched her chin three times as she bought time to consider the offer. She lowered her hand. "Four of my older works and I get to take one that I choose. A total of five." She lifted her eyebrows. "Deal?"

Fen nodded. "Deal." He extended a hand. "Help me up and let me lean on you until we get to my truck."

With the aid of the chair and Bailey, Fen sat, rested for a while, straightened his leg and stood. "It works best if I walk stiff legged for a few days after I've tweaked it."

They made it down the front steps and into the yard before she asked, "How'd you hurt it?"

He spoke through the pain. "A woman shot me."

"Why?"

"I was a highway patrolman, and a constable called for backup. He was trying to serve papers on a woman for removal of her children because of abuse and neglect. She didn't take kindly to the idea of having to go to court."

"I see." She paused. "Wait. I don't understand. If he was serving the papers, why did she shoot you?"

"She was a lousy shot. I was walking toward them and still thirty yards away."

"That stinks!"

Fen's knee flexed, and he almost went down again. He straightened it and took a break from trying to take another step. To keep from thinking about the pain he continued his story. "I thought it was bad luck at the time, but things turned out for the best. My plans to move up in the Highway Patrol went by the wayside, but I had my painting to keep me busy and keep earning decent money. Law enforcement gets in your blood though. I still wanted to follow that dream, so I ran for sheriff." He paused. "That was a joke about running."

Bailey groaned. "Nice one."

"Anyway, they elected me sheriff, which is mainly an administrative job. Everything worked out until Sally..." His words trailed off. "That's a story for another day."

"Tomorrow? On the way to the fair?"

He opened the door to his truck without answering her. "Did you get that new driver's license?"

"It came in the mail on Monday."

"Good. I'll call my insurance agent tonight and get you on my policy. You're driving tomorrow."

Chapter Fifteen

Fen rose from a brief night's sleep at 4:30 a.m. and fit a brace for his knee over blue jeans. He slipped on a jacket and loaded paintings and supplies in the dark. He was grateful for Sam showing up to help, even if he appeared without notice from behind the corner of the garage with only the tent left to pack. Thelma also made a pre-dawn appearance. She presented him with a couple of ham and hard-fried egg sandwiches, along with two thermoses. "One's hot tea and the other's coffee. You and that gal will have to flip a coin to see who gets what."

Fen accepted the care package and mumbled. "It's likely Bailey will take everything and leave me crumbs."

Thelma turned. "I'm liking her and I haven't laid eyes on her yet."

The morning weather forecast came over the truck's speakers. "We're looking at a thirty percent chance of rain today with a better chance tomorrow." Fen shifted his gaze upward and saw low clouds marching in formation.

When he cleared the concrete guardrails on the Brazos

River bridge, the city lights of Springdale, the county seat of Newman County, bounced off clouds scuttling to the northwest. He crossed his fingers and whispered a brief prayer for pleasant weather.

Bugs hovered around the porchlight of Clete's trailer as he pulled off the gravel county road onto a driveway that was more weeds than gravel. Bailey bounded out of the front door with a stack of what he hoped would be the correct number of paintings wrapped in a blanket. He hobble-walked to the passenger's side and said, "I hope you only brought five."

As Bailey moved to the camper shell, she spoke over her shoulder, ignoring his comment and going on offense. "You're late."

"Give an invalid a break, will you? Is your driver's license in your backpack?"

"Do you want to see it, Sheriff Maguire?"

He threw up his hands. "Just asking. Coffee or hot tea?"

"Coffee. Black and strong."

He mumbled under his breath. "That figures. Let's see how hungry she is." He heard the tailgate slam shut and the back window come down with a firm thunk. The overhead light came on as she opened the driver's door. "There's two ham and egg sandwiches for you if you're hungry."

"Yum."

He had his answer, but another question crossed his mind. "Can you eat and drive without wrecking us?"

She gave him a mischievous smile. "I've been hot-wiring cars and taking joy rides since I was thirteen. I'd drink a Dr. Pepper and eat peanuts while I drove around Houston, outrunning every cop in town."

Fen shifted his gaze from her. "Serves me right for asking."

They crossed back over the river bridge, headed west, as Bailey polished off the second sandwich. Fen poured a second cup of coffee into a travel mug, secured the top, and put it in the holder closest to the steering wheel. "Thanks," she said. "This is excellent coffee."

"I'll pass on the compliment to Thelma."

Fen turned toward her. "Is it the coffee buzz, or are you in an exceptionally good mood?"

"Both. I'm an emancipated woman today. Now I don't have to lie for my mother or forge her name."

"What do you mean?"

"I've been signing my mother's name to all sorts of things for years. Texas law is goofy. I had to go to school until I graduated or turned eighteen, but they considered me an adult at seventeen. I could go to prison for committing a felony AND get picked up for skipping school. Crazy, huh?"

"When did you stop stealing cars?"

She cut her eyes to him as her top lip quirked upward. "I abandoned most of my life of crime the day before I turned seventeen. I didn't want to have an adult record."

"Tell me about your mother."

"She and her latest boyfriend kicked me out and told me to come live with Uncle Clete."

"Are you in contact with her?"

She cast a quick gaze his way. "The boyfriend showed me the door, and I was glad to leave. Mom never had that maternal gene you see in Hallmark movies. In a way she did me a favor. Now I know I can make it on my own."

Fen wanted to give her a short lecture about life's disappoints caused by counting unhatched chickens, but refrained. Not only would it make him sound ancient, he remembered how excited he was to earn decent money from selling his works.

The rest of the multi-county trip passed with talk about painting and high expectations for the day. They pulled into the county fairgrounds and parked as close to the site of their booth as the attendant wearing an orange vest allowed. Fen found a young man eager to help Bailey set up the tent for a nominal fee. It took longer because of distance to the site of their booth, but they had everything ready with thirty minutes to spare.

Fen sent Bailey on a breakfast run, and she returned with a box of assorted pastries. It promised to be a great day, despite ominous clouds streaking across the sky. At eleven the rain came down in sheets and the two artists scrambled to unfurl the front cover, zip it shut, and wait out the storm. Unfortunately, the weather forecaster missed the chance of rain by seventy percent and the duration by long hours.

By the time the clouds parted, the fairground was a quagmire. He wondered if Bailey's dreams were as soggy as the walkways. They looked down the aisle of mud puddles with no one but a few vendors wrestling their tents to the ground. Most had already left and any potential customers had long since departed.

"This sucks!" said Bailey as she stomped her foot. "Seven lousy caricatures and five were giveaways to children. Take away the cost of materials and I made about a hundred bucks."

"Plus fifty," said Fen. "I sold one of your paintings."

"Yeah, the one that you didn't want me to bring. You said it wouldn't sell. I set the price at a hundred and you discounted it to fifty. I could have gotten at least seventy-five."

He looked around the tent. "Go find someone I can hire to carry everything to the truck."

"Why can't I drive it in and load it like we did at the Harvest Festival?"

He pointed to the rain saturated ground. "That's not permitted in the agreement I signed. Trucks and cars would sling mud all over the place. Look at all the other vendors, they're carrying their goods and tents to the parking lot."

Bailey stormed out of the shelter and into the muddy aisle. Fen took a seat and waited. He then waited some more. Vendors strode past, some complaining, and others writing the day off with sarcasm and gallows humor.

"No one's here to help for any price," said Bailey with hands on her hips. "What do we do now?"

"We do it ourselves."

She shook her head. "You can barely walk and that parking lot is two miles away."

Fen dismissed the exaggeration with a wave of his hand, and added, "It's less than two hundred yards. Grab as many paintings as you can carry without dropping them and let's go."

Fen's knee screamed for relief by the end of the third trip. He gritted his teeth and trudged through the mud one more time. With the last painting placed in its rack, he locked the back and grabbed his cane. "All we have to do is take down the tent, load it and we'll be out of here."

By the look she gave him, Bailey didn't count this as good news. Once back at the tent, Fen pulled the ties on the back two corners while Bailey attacked the front poles. He hollered over his shoulder. "Make sure you're well back when you undo the last tie." He heard a rush of water, a loud splash, and a string of swear words worthy of the drunk tank at the county jail. He spun to see the damage, his heel caught, and he promptly fell to the ground.

This time Bailey made no move to come to his aid. A quick look confirmed she might as well have stood under a waterfall. He drew blood biting the inside of his top lip, keeping it from betraying the laugh that wanted desperately to escape.

The birthday girl stood shivering. Fen didn't know if it was from the dousing of cold water, or rage at how her day of emancipation had turned out. He swallowed any desire to laugh, pulled himself up to standing with his cane and a tent pole, and looked at Bailey. "You're right. This sucks. Leave the tent. I'll send Sam to get it tomorrow."

She took an oversize breath and set her jaw. "We came with a tent. We'll leave with a tent."

Sweat flowed from Fen by the time the two wrestled the tent down, carried it on their shoulders to the truck, and loaded it. He took a prescription painkiller, swallowed it with tepid leftover tea, and chased the first pill with another. As an afterthought he asked, "Did you get the cash box?"

Bailey's eyes widened. "I thought you did."

Fen pointed to the exit of the fairgrounds parking lot. "I'm not sure if I picked it up or not. It doesn't matter now. It's only money and not that much."

"Easy for you to say."

He pulled a hundred-dollar bill from his wallet and handed it to her. "Stop and get something to eat if you're hungry. I'll be asleep as soon as the pills hit me."

The trip back to the county might have lasted two hours or two days for all Fen knew. He awakened when Bailey punched him hollering, "Wake up."

"Huh? What's wrong?"

"Look, you silly old man. I thought someone was having a bonfire."

Fen shook his head to clear the cobwebs. In the distance he saw yellow flames licking skyward and black smoke rising against a sky cleansed by rain and sporting a full moon. "Hurry," he said in an even voice.

He dragged out his cell phone and punched in 911. The woman answering inquired about the emergency.

"This is Fen Maguire. A single wide trailer is on fire. County Road 314. East of Friendly Baptist Church."

Chapter Sixteen

Flames danced with sparks in an evil tango on the roof of the left side of the trailer. Black smoke funneled upward from a third of the trailer, with more seeping from cracks around the front door. A duct-taped window exploded and a plume of black belched from the cavern and fled skyward.

Bailey slid the truck into the driveway and careened toward the trailer.

"Stop!" Fen's command came at the same instant Bailey slammed on the brakes. She threw her door open the second she put the truck in park and sprinted to the backyard.

Fen slipped his phone in his shirt pocket, yanked the handle, and shouldered the door open. A blast of heat met him. Knives of pain stabbed his knee the second his foot hit the ground. Getting to Bailey was his only concern. But how? He hopped on one foot and tried to take a step. The knee screamed its objection, causing him to shift all his weight to his good leg. He reached down and locked the brace. Like a pirate with a peg-leg, he swung his leg wide, and allowed it to land. Progress was slow and the pain intense, but he trudged on. Bailey's path took him through a wall of smoke and into the backyard.

When he turned the corner, she was already on the back porch. Paintings flew into the yard.

Turning to the trailer, she gripped the doorknob and screamed. It was a cry like Fen had never heard before, blending physical agony and the deepest soul-pain imaginable. He thought he heard her cry out for her daddy, but it could have been something else. All the while he made steady progress to her with his newfound swing, plant, hop, method of running.

"Get out!" he hollered. The fire answered with crackles, hisses, and moans that sounded like sadistic laughter. A wave of black smoke swept over the porch. Sounds of deep coughing cut through the riot of the fire. He could no longer see Bailey, only hear her coughing.

He jerked so hard on the screen door that it separated from its hinges and fell to the grass below. The smoke eased enough that he could make out her form, and then a breeze carried it away so he could see clearly. A fresh odor lodged in his brain. Burnt flesh. Something else, too. Was it gasoline or diesel? No time to waste.

Bailey sat on the wooden deck facing the trailer, unmoving, and looking at the doorknob where she'd left a strip of skin on the super-heated knob.

Another window exploded and a cloud of boiling smoke made a direct assault. Fen tried not to breathe, but there was no escape, and no time to waste. He reached down and grabbed the back of Bailey's jeans, lifted her, and flung her through the open door into the backyard. He crawled to where she lay and turned her over. A blank stare greeted him. This only lasted a moment as she expelled smoke from her lungs. Tears made streaks down her soot-covered face.

"We have to move," he said in a voice he tried to calm. "You can't give up. I won't let you."

A flicker of wanting to live came back to her, and she nodded. But it was only a flicker. She rose and staggered to the corner of the trailer that was not yet fully engulfed in flames.

"Hey," shouted Fen. "What about me?"

She kept walking, coughing as she went.

By now Fen knew he could make it to the front yard if he got on his feet. He rolled to a discarded riding lawn mower and used his arms and good leg until he stood upright. It was there he picked up a single painting of Bailey's. He then hopped and swung his bad leg until he made it to the front of the trailer.

Bailey sat on her bicycle with her right hand on the handlebar and her left dangling.

"We need to move the truck before it catches fire," said Fen.

She stared at the flames. "My bicycle."

"Leave it."

"It's all... I own." Coughing racked her again.

Fen stood in front of her and tried to coax her to get in the truck. It did no good. The fire had hypnotized her. She looked through him into the merciless flames.

He took her by the shoulders and shook her. The heat from the conflagration heated his back until he thought his shirt might catch fire. As a last resort, he slapped her. He did it again, harder.

Her head shook. "Stop, Momma!" She looked down at her left hand, screamed, and swung her leg up and over the bicycle seat. It fell to the ground.

"Get in the truck. The paint on the hood is bubbling."

She complied, but got in the passenger's seat. This left him with but one thing to do. He hobbled and hopped to the driver's side, used the steering wheel to pull himself up, started the truck, and threw it in reverse with the door open. Luckily, the truck was on an incline and it rolled back toward the road. Once on packed gravel, he put the truck in park, released the hinge on the brace and cried out as he forced his leg to bend. Only then could he pull both legs in and shut the driver's door.

Bailey's small body racked with deep coughing. He joined her in fighting for breaths that felt like someone had put stinging nettle in his throat and lungs.

After clearing tears from his eyes, he used his hands to adjust his injured leg, made sure it wasn't anywhere near the accelerator, and put the truck in gear. Smoke-seared eyes, stabbing pain, coughing spasms, and the strange sensation of using his left foot to operate the brake and gas pedal made it difficult to concentrate on what he needed to do. At least he could give his phone a voice command to call the hospital. The call went through and they promised to be ready for an incoming burn victim.

His hacking cough indicated that two people would need treatment.

As he passed the small church, a deputy's SUV screamed past him with lights activated and siren howling into the night. The first fire truck sped past him as he approached the city limit sign. So much for a swift response on Halloween. He then remembered a carnival at the primary school. Giving rides on the town's shiny red vehicles had delayed their response.

Between coughs, he thought about what else he needed to do. Thinking ahead was something he always prided himself on, but the fits of coughing made concentration almost impossible. Finally, he dug his phone out of his pocket again and told it to call Chuck Forsythe.

"Hey, buddy. Happy Halloween! How were sales?"

Fen didn't have the ability or inclination for small talk. A coughing spasm hit him before he could speak. After fighting for breath, he whispered, "Bailey. Burned bad. Hospital."

Attendants met them with a wheelchair. He had Bailey's window down and tried to holler for her to wake up, but his voice came out weak and scratchy. The scrubs-clad attendants didn't need to be told what to do. Bailey's head lolled from side to side. Was she alive or dead? Through stinging eyes, he saw a blurred vision of them speeding her toward the door on a gurney.

Fen rested his head on the steering wheel. Pain kept him from slipping into a deep slumber. He didn't know how long he stayed in that position, but roused when his door opened. The deep voice of a man said, "Come on, Sheriff. Let's get you inside so our new intern can check you out." He wore deep blue scrubs and Fen recognized him as a man he'd given a break to for an expired inspection sticker and speeding.

The man had arms as thick as Fen's thighs but a touch gentle enough to get him in a wheelchair with only a few stabbing pains. The attendant's name tag read John Smith. "Funny," said Fen. "I know your face. Couldn't remember John Smith."

The man's laugh boomed across the parking lot. "There aren't too many of us around these days since men decided they could call themselves something they think sounds cool, like Gangsta-Q, or Rap-R-Man. I'm thinking about calling my boy Lay-Z if he doesn't get off the couch and get a job."

Fen chuckled, which brought on a coughing attack.

"If as much smoke is in you as what's on you, we'd best get you inside, Sheriff."

"My truck. Don't want it towed."

"I'll move it, make sure it's locked, and bring the keys to you."

Fen nodded his appreciation.

What happened next was an absolute blur of activity. His shirt succumbed to a flashing pair of scissors. A plastic mask went over his nose and he felt a prick from a needle going into his arm. All he could see of his assailants were eyes above blue and white masks and what looked like pajamas. The air coming through the mask was cool, as was his skin after being washed with tepid water and soap.

Then things slowed. People disappeared. The curtains were all around his bed and he was alone, with only mechanical beeps and the barely audible hiss of oxygen. His leg throbbed, but the ice pack helped dull the pain. A woman came in with a syringe in her hand. She moved to the IV stand, uncapped the needle and stabbed it into a port in the tube leading to his hand.

"How's Bailey?" he said into the plastic.

The woman's eyes didn't give away anything. "Don't you worry about her. She's a fighter."

"What did you give me?"

"Something to make you stop asking questions." She winked. "Count backward from thirty."

Fen ignored the instruction. His last two thoughts were questions. Who did Bailey cry out for on the back porch, and who set fire to the trailer?

Chapter Seventeen

Disoriented to time, day, and place, Fen tried to open eyelids that didn't want to separate. He raised a hand to force them open and drew back fingers covered with a gooey substance. His nose itched and a quick check revealed the reason. Cool oxygen flowed through a plastic tube into his nostrils. The familiar voice of a man said, "They put some sort of medicated petroleum jelly on your face and eyes. You look like you fell asleep on the beach."

Fen gave his head a nod. He tried to speak, but nothing came out on the first attempt. He gave it a second attempt and said, "Water."

Chuck Forsythe smiled down at him. "Glad to see you, too. I'll call the nurse."

Fen grabbed Chuck's arm. "Bailey?"

A comforting hand patted the one that gripped Chuck. "She's alive. They transferred her last night."

"Where?"

"Houston, but don't worry about that now. She's getting first class care."

It wasn't long before a nurse held a straw to Fen's lips. The first sip was cold enough to have come from a mountain stream's snow melt. Ice made little crunching sounds as it shifted in the cup.

"Better?" asked the nurse.

Fen nodded.

"Drink all you want. Cold water will soothe that scratchy throat."

He took the oversized plastic mug from her with the hand not encumbered with tubes and tried to say thank you with his eyes. After a few more sips, he leaned back into the pillow. It had to be the best water he'd ever tasted. Then he tested his lungs with a deeper breath of air. A hacking cough followed.

The nurse didn't seem concerned. "That should go away in a few days. Your blood-oxygen level is good, but the doctor wants you to breathe the good stuff until it gets a little higher. Once that happens, you can go home."

Fen wanted to try out his voice again, so he took several sips of ice water to dull the discomfort. "How long?"

It felt like someone had worked over his vocal cords with a rasp, but his words came out stronger and clearer.

The nurse shook her head. "I knew you'd be like this. Can't wait to get out there and play cops and robbers."

"No more cops and robbers. Besides, I don't like hospital food."

She tilted her head. "Listen to you jabber. I'd better leave before you burst into song."

Chuck gave a scoffing laugh. "I've heard him sing. It qualifies as cruel and unusual punishment to anyone who hears it."

The nurse left and Fen motioned for Chuck to come close. "Is Bailey going to make it?"

The attorney gave his head a nod. "It's hard to get information, but I heard them say she was in stable condition and her injuries weren't life threatening. It's her hand, more than her lungs, even though she took in a lot of smoke."

A wave of partial relief swept over Fen. Bailey would live, but what about the burns? He replayed the sound of her scream and winced.

Chuck's voice broke through the replay of the fire and caused him to focus. "You need to tell me what happened before Lori barges in."

Fen stiffened. "Lori? She's here?"

"She's been here most of the night. I told her she couldn't talk to you. As your attorney, I recommend we hold off saying anything until I get the story from you. Are you up to telling me what happened?"

A nod of his head preceded his words. "Do they suspect me of setting the fire?"

"If you were still sheriff, what would you think?"

"I'd be a suspect." Fen took a sip of water. "I'll talk as long as my voice holds out."

The story began when Bailey roused Fen from his slumber on their trip home and he saw smoke and flames rising in the distance. Regular swallows of water calmed his throat so he could relate details.

Chuck listened to the entire story before he asked, "You're positive it was arson?"

"It had to be, and I believe it started in the master bedroom. I smelled some sort of petroleum product on the back porch and it went up like a roman candle after the flames hit it." A revelation hit Fen. "I need you to get the keys to my truck. In the back seat, there's one of Bailey's paintings that she threw in the backyard. I grabbed it before the porch went up in a huge fireball. Get it to Tom Stevens and have him send it to the state lab in Austin. They'll be able to tell what kind of accelerant the arsonist used."

A smile parted Chuck's lips. "I'm glad that fire didn't cook your brain."

Fen responded with a smile of his own.

A knock on the door preceded it opening. With tentative steps, Lori entered the room and shut the door behind her. "Hello, James Fenimore Maguire."

She came to his bedside and took his hand. She hadn't called him by his entire name since before he told Lori's father of his insistence on honoring Sally's desire not to pursue a second heart transplant. Lori, the kid sister to Sally, used his full name as a title of endearment. It was like a funny nickname and only she used it. A way of teasing him and daring him to correct her.

His mouth opened to speak, but only a squeak came.

"Don't talk," said Lori as a tear slid down her cheek. "I only came by to tell you... well, what I mean is... uh. Oh, never mind James Fenimore, you know what I'm trying to say."

He tried to swallow the lump in his throat, but without water to pave the way, he lapsed into a coughing fit. When he looked up, all he saw of Lori was her quick step into the hall.

Chuck's eyebrows shot upward when Fen looked at him. "That's not what I was expecting from her."

Fen returned to his plastic insulated glass and straw. He swallowed several cold drinks and meditated in silence.

After Chuck looked at his watch, Fen knew his friend needed to go. With a hand raised, Fen said, "Ask Tom to find out who's investigating the fire. Also, do you know for sure who owns the land and trailer?"

"I believe it's Nathaniel Newman, but I'll have Candy go to the courthouse today and double check."

The morning passed with cool oxygen coming through the mask and water soothing Fen's throat. By noon he was ready to pull out the I.V. At one o'clock the nurse did that very thing, along with removing the oxygen. "The doctor ordered your release two hours ago. That's why you didn't get lunch."

Fen choked down a sarcastic reply as Thelma burst into the room. She took one look at Fen and shook her head. "Get dressed. The day's half over and it's time you did something besides lay around. Or are you now a man of leisure?"

He looked at her but didn't feel the question deserved an answer. Instead, he tried to get a step ahead of his housekeeper and cook. "Did Sam come with you?"

"How else did you think we were going to get you and your truck home?" She hefted a carry-on size bag to the foot of the bed, barely missing his sore knee. "There's clean underwear, socks, that ugly T-shirt you like so much, house shoes, and warm-up pants in there. I was going to bring jeans, but decided against it after I spoke with that lawyer. He's all right, but everyone knows it's his wife that does all the work."

Fen looked at the nurse. "Do you see what I have to put up with?"

Instead of responding to Fen, the nurse looked at Thelma. "He'll have more pain in his leg than anything else. We're sending him home with a prescription for something that will make him loopy. You know the routine. Keep him off that bad leg, ice it, and cram anti-inflammatory over-the-counter pills down him, as directed."

"You're preaching to the choir," said Thelma. "I've been nursing that bad knee for years. Tell me, is it true what I'm hearing about Lilly Boggs? Is she really going to retire?"

Fen watched as the two women left the room, talking over each other like birds on a fence line. He might as well have been a two-week-old sale flier from the local grocery store. It wasn't easy, but he wrestled on the clothes, except for the socks, and waited for someone to bring a wheelchair. That occurred ten minutes later.

Sam waited with the passenger door to Fen's truck open. The wheelchair cleared the front doors of the hospital, but forward progress slowed to a crawl. In his path stood the reporter for the local newspaper. Even in his drug-induced haze, Fen could see the determination in Lou Cooper's eyes.

"Mr. Maguire, what caused the fire?"

"You'll need to ask the police."

"Was the trailer already on fire when you and Bailey Madison arrived?"

"Yes."

"Where had you two been all day?"

Fen clamped his teeth together.

"I have multiple reports that you'd gone to a Halloween Fair to sell yours and Bailey's paintings. Is that correct?"

"It seems you already know enough to write your story."

"Bailey received significant burns to her hand and smoke inhalation. How did that happen?"

Fen finally made it to the curb. "There was a fire. That's how she sustained injuries."

The reporter let out a huff and lowered her voice to a more secretive volume. She grabbed the arms of the wheelchair. "I've done this type of reporting for a long time, and I smell a big story. First, it was the murder of Cletus Brumbaugh. Then drugs were found in Nathaniel Newman's truck. Then, a deputy almost died and there wasn't anyone to back him up."

She wasn't finished. "Now someone torched Mr. Newman's trailer. Clete Brumbaugh's niece, who just happened to live in that trailer is seriously injured, and you were with her. You found Clete's body, and you reported the fire. Either this is a bizarre coincidence, someone's trying to set you up, trying to pin the crimes on Nathaniel Newman, or you have something to hide."

Fen looked her in the eye. "Which do you think?"

She didn't budge, and his stare didn't seem to faze her. "I don't know what to think. This story isn't going away and neither am I. This is your chance to get ahead of the rumors that are flying. The quicker the truth is told, the sooner you can get back to your new job and stop pretending all you do is paint."

He looked up. She had big, brown, inquisitive eyes. "What does that mean?"

"It means I know you have a private investigator's license. That's newsworthy, and it's going in the next edition unless I get something with some meat on the bones."

Fen hated himself for applying for the license on a whim. If he didn't head her off, Lou Cooper would have his photo on the front page, exactly where he didn't want it to be. He wondered if he could use this reporter's curiosity to his advantage.

He cleared his scratchy throat. "I tell you what, Ms. Cooper. Give me a week to mend and we'll talk."

She shook her shoulder-length brown hair, sprinkled with strands of gray. "I need something before then. Right now, your involvement in the case is the best story I have."

"How soon do you need something?"

"Today works for me."

He shook his head. "Three days from now."

"I'll give you until tomorrow."

"Don't get greedy. I'll know more in three days. You can come for supper."

"One day, but I'll settle for a first-hand account of the fire. We'll negotiate the rest of the story later."

"Two days. That still gives you time to meet your deadline."

She released her grip on the wheelchair, taking the scent of her perfume with her. "Don't stand me up, Mr. Maguire. My words can either be your friend, or your worst enemy."

"Dinner. My place. Monday evening at six thirty." He extended a hand.

They exchanged a firm handshake and Lou took off at a quick walk.

Sam stood by the truck, looking down. "You'll be sorry."

"I can handle her," said Fen as he pushed himself up from the wheelchair.

Sam looked at Lou's shapely form as she strode to her car. "Not her," said Sam. "You have to tell Thelma to cook for another woman."

Fen mumbled, "Should have told Lou to pick up burgers and meet me under the bridge."

Sam walked to the driver's side without offering to assist him into the truck. Except for forcing his leg to bend, the transition from wheelchair to vehicle went with only moderate pain. Once settled with his seat belt fastened, Sam said, "Thelma found your walker in the garage. She says you'll use it until you can walk better."

"Not a bad idea, at least until the swelling goes down."

Fen didn't speak again until they approached the river bridge. "What do you think about that room over the garage? I mean, Bailey doesn't have a place to live anymore, and it's been converted to a studio apartment."

Sam grunted before he spoke. "Thelma said you need to make her a bedroom, leave the kitchen and bathroom like they are and make an art studio for the girl out of the rest."

Fen cut his eyes toward Sam. "Any other instructions from Thelma?"

Another grunt from Sam that he interpreted as something else for Fen to do. "No more high school. Help her get a GED."

"I'll think about that one."

Sam shrugged. "She won't go back."

Fen didn't say it, but he knew Thelma and Sam were right.

Bailey had a different path to follow than most. Her school days ended when she grabbed the doorknob of a trailer set ablaze by someone he would find and bring to justice. For now, he and Bailey needed to heal. In two days, he'd meet with a pushy newspaper reporter and find out how much she knew while playing his own cards close to his vest.

He smiled. At least, that was his plan. Sometimes his plans worked, and other times... not so much.

Chapter Eighteen

Painting while sitting didn't suit Fen, but he soldiered through and squirted another dollop of buff titanium with burnt sienna, giving an additional hue to his current work in progress. The door and walls of his studio were no match for Thelma's piercing voice.

"Mr. Fen. That hussy is here again."

Fen shook his head and hollered back. "Can you be more specific?"

The door opened. "It's that Danni woman who thinks she's ready for a part on television playing a crime scene investigator. If you ask me, she's looking to play the wife of someone I know in real life."

Fen kept working the colors together. "Have her come in and bring us something to drink."

"You shouldn't be having company so soon after leaving the hospital. I'll tell her you're not up to it."

Fen gave her a stare that communicated he wasn't buying what Thelma was trying to sell.

She threw up her hands. "It's your funeral. I swear, you're

the second most hard-headed man I've ever laid eyes on. Sam's the worst, but I expect that from him. It's you that doesn't have an excuse."

"Get the door," said Fen.

"I'll get it, but you keep one hand on your wallet. I know a gold digger when I see one."

After Thelma left, Fen considered her mini-tirade. It didn't last as long as most. He wondered if she was warming up to Danni.

The door opened as Fen filled his brush with a color that would give fall leaves a desire to release from their branches and cartwheel to the ground. At least that was the look he was going for. He stayed focused on his brush strokes. "Come in, Danni. I've been thinking of you all day."

Danni moved into the periphery of his field of vision. "Is that a fact? I didn't expect such a compliment."

Fen chuckled. "I probably should have said I've been wondering if you found anything interesting at the crime scene."

"Other than it was arson?"

He loaded his brush again, moved to a different portion of the canvas, and applied strokes that were softer than the first. He pulled back his brush and examined his work. "It helps to stand back from time to time to see if you're blurring the less important details into the background."

With a nod of confidence, Fen pointed with his brush as he leaned back. "There. See how the tree to the left of the center almost comes at you, but the one to the right fades into the others beside it? It's kind of like clues in an investigation. Some will stand out and others melt away."

Danni laughed. "Did that fire cook your brain or is philosophy a new hobby of yours? Did you hear me? We've ruled the trailer fire arson."

Fen wiped his brush and placed it in a cup of solvent. "That was never in doubt, was it?"

"I guess not, but I always get jazzed when I discover the type of accelerant used and where the fire started. I also found something that might break the case wide open."

Thelma arrived and passed out drinks without a word.

Danni thanked her, and Thelma gave a nod but no smile. Fen sipped and waited until the door closed again and Danni told him why she really came to see him on this windy Monday afternoon. She'd downed half the glass when she set it on the table with more paint than plastic showing. "I need some advice, but I don't know how to ask you for it."

Fen raised a single brow. "I've found that using words works better than anything else I've tried."

She threw her head back and laughed. "I guess that's why you were sheriff and I'm a lowly crime scene investigator." Her countenance darkened. "I'm serious. This involves some of the most influential people in the county, and I believe there's enough evidence for an arrest."

"What about a conviction?" asked Fen.

"It's possible."

Fen took another drink of tea. "I don't want you to get into trouble by discussing an ongoing investigation with someone who's not in law enforcement. You'll need to choose your words with care. No names. Pretend you're telling a made-up story that occurred someplace else."

"Do you want me to say, *Once upon a time?*"

"That's not a bad idea."

Danni gave her head a sharp nod. "Once upon a time, there was a very rich man who lived far, far away. He had money, land, cattle, oil, and much sway over what happened in his corner of the world."

Fen closed his eyes as Danni continued. "This rich man did

things his way. The older he grew, the more he demanded people obey his commands. If they didn't, he had ways of dealing with them. It's said that he had a man killed and then burned that man's home."

Fen opened his eyes. "Could the reeve over the shire prove any of this?"

Her head tilted. "What's a reeve?"

"It's an old English word. The reeve was the administrative agent of the king. It was his responsibility to enforce the edicts of the king in a designated area called a shire, very similar to our counties. He was the shire's reeve."

Danni looked at the ceiling. "I get it. The sheriff."

"Just a bit of trivia. Get back to your story."

"In this story, the shire's reeve and the rich landowner are blood kin." She separated her next words. "Very... closely... related."

"Ah. I understand. That is a delicate situation. The person with information about the killing and burning of the home is concerned the shire's reeve will protect the close relative and possibly retaliate against anyone who brings accusations against the wealthy man."

"Exactly."

Fen rocked back and forth as he thought. He stopped rocking and took up the story where Danni left off. "In that same distant land, there's an invention called a printing press. From time to time, people discussed stories with the owner of the printing press. He'd print them, but he was a person of sound character and never revealed his sources of information. Over time, and it took a long time, stories came forth about the rich man. At first, they only hinted at misdeeds. As time went on, more and more facts came to light. Eventually, the king read the stories. He sent knights into the land to confront the shire's reeve about why the rich man wasn't held to account for his crimes."

Danni stayed silent for a long time. "That sounds like a wonderful story, but wasn't it dangerous for the people who gave stories to the man with the printing press?"

"Of course."

"Wasn't there anyone in the shire that was stouthearted enough to supply the king with information? Perhaps the man who used to be reeve over the shire?"

Fen gave his head a firm, negative shake. "Alas, the former reeve retired to a life of writing sonnets. He'd had his day in the sun and wanted nothing more than a quill, ink, and parchment. Besides, a wench threw a dagger at her husband, missed, and took down the former reeve. The wound healed poorly."

Danni ran a finger around the rim of her glass. "Does this tale have a happy ending?"

After tugging on his chin like it had long whiskers, Fen dropped his hand. "The people of the shire had to learn to not count on the old, injured reeve. They had to take risks themselves."

"Thanks, Fen. Your story makes sense."

He held up his hands. "Don't forget, all I plan on doing is limp around the house and paint. You'll need to decide what part you play." He paused. "Unless I'm wrong, you have hero blood in your veins and you know other heroes."

FEN SPENT the rest of the afternoon painting and thinking. There was no doubt that Danni had gathered evidence that would point to Nathaniel Newman as the person behind the killing of Clete Brumbaugh. She must have found something in the ashes of the trailer to implicate him in that crime too. But what? He wished he could sift through the remains to see if she'd missed anything, but his leg and prior dinner commitment with Lou Cooper wouldn't allow a late night visit to the remains of the trailer. Besides, he needed to be rested for his trip tomorrow to Houston to see Bailey.

"Patience," he whispered to himself. "Things are moving faster, and it won't be long before my father-in-law feels the heat."

Fen cleaned his brushes, but did nothing else to make his studio look any more presentable. Why would he? He wasn't trying to impress a pushy newspaper reporter, even though he allowed himself plenty of time to shower, shave, and put on a collared shirt.

Lou rang the doorbell at six thirty sharp. Thelma hollered from the kitchen. "Get the door! I'm up to my elbows in biscuit dough."

Fen knew it had more to do with Thelma's aversion to women coming into Sally's prior domain. He understood her reluctance, but the passive aggressive behavior had worn thin after a year. Pulling himself up on his walker, he shuffled the best he could to the front door.

Before him stood Lou, wearing jeans, rubber boots, and a Dallas Cowboys sweatshirt two sizes too big. She'd piled her hair up on her head in a messy bun with an ink pen impaled in it. Her face was void of makeup.

"Forgive the appearance," she said. "I'm supplementing my income by freelance writing and time got away from me." She looked at the walker. "Don't move yet. I need to slip off these boots before I come in. I don't want Thelma throwing me out before I've interviewed you."

Fen held the walker steady as Lou gripped it with one hand and pried her boots off with the other. While she tugged, Fen asked, "Do you always write wearing rubber boots?"

She laughed as she righted herself and slipped on a pair of houseshoes. "After I finished the first draft, I harvested the last crop from my fall garden. Hence, the boots. I thought I had more time."

Fen took a step back until Lou said, "Wait. We need to talk before we go in."

"We do?"

Lou nodded. "I did some snooping on you, Thelma, and Sam. It's Thelma that has me worried."

"She rarely bites."

"That's not what I hear, and I need her on my side, or at least neutral. She's a woman of significant influence in certain circles. I can't afford for her to poison the well, so to speak, with sources I'm looking to develop."

Fen tilted his head. "What can I do? She's an independent thinker."

"And she has a quick tongue."

Fen nodded. "I can't deny that."

Lou's tone lowered to that of a conspirator. "Thelma grieved almost as much as you did when you lost your wife. The grapevine has it she doesn't like women to sit at your dining room table. Is there any way we can eat somewhere else? Maybe a breakfast nook?"

Fen scratched his chin. "It adjoins the kitchen, and that's where Sally and I had breakfast most every morning. Now, it's Thelma's domain. Sometimes she won't let me in there. We could eat on the back patio."

"Perfect. You go to the back patio and I'll speak to Thelma."

Fen wondered when he lost control of his home, but had to admit, the idea of eating on the neutral ground of the back patio was a way to avoid his cook's looks of disapproval when she served their meal. He stopped at the living room, and pointed at a hall. "Formal dining room, and then the kitchen."

He made it to the back door and opened it. Instead of stepping onto the patio, he shut the door with a resounding thud and backtracked through the living room. A bump-out hid him from the formal dining room where he waited and listened.

The sound of the kitchen door opened. He heard, "Thelma? Fen sent me to tell you something."

"What does that man want now?"

"He wants to know if it's alright if we eat on the patio instead of in the formal dining room."

Thelma's voice grew louder. She must've stepped into the dining room. "He don't want to eat in here?"

Instead of answering, Lou asked a question of her own. "Is this a portrait of Fen's wife?"

"That's Miss Sally. Best woman that ever took a breath."

"She's absolutely stunning. I don't think I've ever seen a more perfect complexion. Is this really what she looked like?"

"Open that top drawer to the sideboard and pull out her photograph. All Mr. Fen did was paint what was there."

The sound of a drawer opening reached Fen. Next, Lou asked, "Was she as sweet as people say?"

"Miss Lou, she was good through and through."

Fen needed to swallow, but feared a croak or moan would give away his eavesdropping, so he held it in.

"I think," Lou hesitated. "I think you should leave this room as is. You know, something like a shrine to Miss Sally. It almost seems like a crime to eat in here."

"I've been trying to tell Mr. Fen that very thing. Some things are meant to be left alone."

A barrage of words came from Thelma that detailed items in the room that Sally had selected. Fen used the ramblings to cover his escape. He plopped down on a padded chair and marveled. In less than five minutes, Lou had endeared herself to the most overprotective and opinionated woman in the county. Information would flow after Thelma gave her approval for her tribe to speak to the newspaper reporter.

All it cost Fen was the use of his formal dining room. He wondered how he could settle the score for losing a place to eat. An idea came to mind. Lou had her brief victory. It would soon be time for him to play for bigger stakes.

Chapter Nineteen

Thelma cleared the plates from the glass-topped table on the patio as Fen and Lou moved from the wicker chairs to a pair of cushioned lawn chairs. On the way he detoured to the fire pit and flipped a switch. Flames rose from fake logs.

"Nice trick," said Lou.

"I designed it as a wood-burner, but the smoke swirled on the porch and Thelma threw a fit about smoke stinking up the house every time someone opened the door. We compromised and I'm glad we did."

Lou cast her gaze upon the river valley below. "This is quite a place. I understand it was a wedding present."

"The land was. Everything else Sally and I paid for, as we had the money." Fen pointed at Thelma's tiny home behind the garage. "That was the first thing we built. I was a highway patrolman, and Sally taught at the high school." He threw a thumb over his shoulder. "We dreamed big when we designed the house, without a clue how we'd pay for it. Then my paintings started to sell."

He shifted his gaze from the river to Lou. "I have that newspaper you worked for in Dallas to thank for my success. They ran a piece in the Sunday paper about an artist state trooper. I guess it was the novelty that caught people's eye."

Lou kept her gaze fixed on a distant spot. "I remember the story. It came out when I was trying to beat rival newspapers with a scoop on a triple homicide. Little did I know it wasn't the other reporters I needed to worry about. My second ex-husband worked for the other major newspaper. He took all the information I'd gathered, wrote the story, and took full credit for it."

"I can see how that would make for an awkward conversation."

"It wasn't awkward. Just loud." She pointed at the fire. "I put everything he owned in the dumpster of our townhouse complex, soaked it with gasoline, threw in a lit match, and drove away to an efficiency apartment I'd rented."

"That should have been easy for the cops to figure out. How much trouble did you get into?"

"He was in Vegas with a young lady who looked older than what her learner's permit stated. Dallas P.D. didn't seem interested in a little dumpster fire after the girl's parents filed charges against him."

It surprised Fen how open Lou was in revealing a painful chapter of her life. Was it idle conversation, or would she expect something in return? He pressed her. "You said that was your second husband. What happened to the first?"

She let out a sigh. "The same thing that happened to all three. Being an average reporter isn't hard. Becoming a good reporter is more difficult, and it's almost impossible to be recognized as a great reporter. They say those reporters have ink in their veins instead of blood. I wanted a full transfusion. The long and short of my marriages is that I was a bigamist. It took three marriages for me to figure out I couldn't be married to my job and to a man at the same time." She kept looking at the river. "Go ahead. Ask me why the newspaper let me go."

"All right. Why?"

"Times changed, and I didn't change with them. I reported the truth and didn't pull punches. I pounded on the editor's desk and fought for my stories." She let out a huff. "That used to work for me. It was a corruption story that sealed my fate. They spiked it and then fired me for not producing usable stories."

"Ah," was Fen's only response.

She shifted her gaze to look at him. "How did you manage being a state trooper, a well-respected sheriff, an artist whose works sell in the tens of thousands, and a good husband?"

He turned his head to face her. Amber light from the fire cast a glow over one side of her face. Fen collected his thoughts. "I'm not sure what kind of answer you're looking for."

Her voice held the curiosity of a scientist looking for an answer to a question that had puzzled her for years. "Everyone I've talked to about you and Sally says you had a storybook marriage. No one can recall either of you not showing respect and admiration for the other. What was your secret?"

Fen squirmed in his seat. Lou was nobody's fool so he'd best not try to deceive her. Still, he needed to get the conversation off of him as soon as possible.

"Off the record?" he asked.

"Are we going to play that game?"

"The details of our marriage are off limits to the public."

Lou stared into the flames for several seconds. "I should know by now that people think and act in ways that are foreign to me. It was a selfish question. Curiosity is my strength and my curse. My forte is to report hard, gritty stories where people get hurt and there are few winners. Forget I asked about your marriage."

Fen rubbed his knee, more out of habit than it hurting. "I didn't say I wouldn't answer your question. All I ask is that I don't read about it."

Lou issued her first smile of the evening. "I'll make an exception. Whatever you say about your marriage to Sally is off the record."

Fen held up his right index finger. "Number one. We talked every morning before we went our separate ways, and every night we made a point to talk about our day."

"Every morning and night?"

"We never missed a day. Sometimes we had to get creative, but we spoke twice. Mornings we discussed what we planned to do, and the evenings we talked about what we'd done. It was a time commitment we made in an effort to stay connected."

His middle finger joined his index finger. "Number two habit. Whenever we had a big decision, we prayed and didn't move forward until we agreed."

"Tell me you're joking. I didn't have you pegged as a holy roller."

Fen shook his head. "Don't look now, but your bias is showing."

"Prayer didn't save your wife, and now you don't attend church. It looks like you gave up on God after he didn't perform for you."

A stab of loss hit Fen under the rib cage. He'd felt it before and knew he'd experience it again. After gathering his emotions, he looked at Lou. "It took me a long time to understand what Sally was saying. She wanted to live, but she couldn't deprive someone of their first new heart when she'd already had one. I'm at peace with our decision, and it doesn't matter to me what you think or say about it. As for praying, I never gave up on God. He's helping me get through losing the most precious person any man could want."

Fen sat up straight. "I've changed my mind. Print what I said. Just make sure you quote me accurately."

It was either a reflection from the fire, or Lou's brown eyes had moistened.

Fen had one more thing to say about Sally. "It might interest your readers to know that I still talk to Sally every morning. I have her ashes in an urn in my study."

"Look, Fen. I'm sorry." Lou shook her head. "I have no right to mock your beliefs. I shouldn't compare your life to mine. It seems the men I'm attracted to weren't interested in daily talks and I never took the time. Perhaps things would have turned out different if I'd not been so wrapped up in myself."

She glanced over at him. "What about at night?"

"Huh?"

"You said you speak with Sally every morning. Do you still talk to her each night?"

"Not anymore. Don't need to, because I talk to her when I paint. By the time I'm finished for the day, I'm out of words."

The back door creaked open. "You two ready for coffee and dessert, or are you going to stare at that fire a while longer?"

Fen craned his neck. "Coffee and dessert sounds good to me."

"Perfect," said Lou. "If I'm going to blow my diet, I might as well go all the way."

"Coming right up," said Thelma as she shut the door.

Lou turned around to face the fire. "She's something else. Where did you find her?"

"County jail." The answer came out like jail was the most natural place to find a cook and housekeeper. "She did six months after beating a man with a metal pitcher. He made fun of her name. Sally would come to jail if we had female prisoners and lead a bible study. She got to know Thelma and insisted we hire her." He tilted his head. "Have you heard her husband's story yet?"

"I didn't know she was married."

"Go back through the newspaper's archives if you run out of things to do. Two sheriffs ago, they convicted Sam of voluntary manslaughter. After my first election, he wrote a letter asking me to look into his case. To make a long story short, I did. It turns out he had an air-tight alibi and my predecessor suppressed evidence in the original trial. Now he's my farm manager."

Lou tapped a fingernail on the arm of her chair. "That might make a good follow-up story."

"Good luck with that. He got burned by your newspaper during his original trial, and they weren't even-handed during the appeal process. He thinks it's because he's a Choctaw Indian."

"So, you not only helped get him released, but you hired him when he was released from prison."

"Why not? He's a rancher, farmer, and a one-man security system." Fen pointed to the river bottom. "He's somewhere out there... probably watching us."

She shook her head. "I bet he's in their little house watching a football game."

"You'd be wrong. The porch light isn't on."

"What's that supposed to mean?"

Fen looked into the darkness. "That's a story for another day."

With the heavy talk about Sally, and enough said concerning Thelma and Sam, he changed his voice to sound more upbeat. "Why don't you drive me to Houston tomorrow morning?"

Her head jerked around. "To see Bailey?"

"I spoke with her doctor this afternoon and received permission to visit."

"How is she? Are her injuries as serious as people are saying? Did you ask if I can talk to her?"

"Slow down. Bailey's eighteen. She can talk to anyone she wants."

Lou looked at her shoes and then brought her gaze back to him. "She can also refuse to talk to anyone and everyone."

Fen nodded. "That's one reason we're going together. I'll try to run interference for you, but it will be her decision to speak with you or not. However, I do have a favor to ask."

A narrowing of the eyelids told him she was on her guard. "A favor?"

"She doesn't know it yet, but I'm renovating a place for her over the garage. I'd like you to take photos of it tonight to show her. It's already a studio apartment with a miniature kitchen and a full bathroom. I'm dividing it into a bedroom and her own studio."

"I don't get it," said Lou. "Why do you want me to play show and tell with Bailey?"

Fen drug his hand down his face. "We didn't exactly have a great day together on Halloween. She's a handful on a good day, and that may have been the worst day of her life. She needs to talk about what happened and you're the queen of questions."

Lou cocked her head. "I'm not sure how to take that last statement. Was it intended as a jab or a compliment?"

Fen waved off the question. "Bailey's a tough kid who needs someone just as tough."

"You realize I'm a reporter and not a therapist, don't you?"

"She'd tell a therapist to take a hike. All I'm asking is that you look at her situation objectively and give her options. I think she'll choose wisely as long as she's not pressured. She'll come and live here if she thinks with her head and not her feelings."

Thelma came through the back door with a tray topped by two pieces of carrot cake and two cups of coffee. She lowered the tray so Lou could take her dessert plate and mug. "If you want more, there's plenty, Miss Lou."

She made the same delivery to Fen without the offer of a second helping. "Don't ask, Mr. Fen. You're getting thick around the middle since you acted like a fool and made it so you can't ride that bicycle that goes nowhere."

Fen knew better than to reply. Thelma would see it as an invitation to spar and he might not finish his conversation with Lou. It only took three minutes for Thelma to receive and respond to enough compliments that she went indoors.

Once they'd dispatched the spicy cake with the decadent icing, Fen got back to business. "There are a couple of things you need to know about the fire."

"Hold on. Let me get out my notepad and pen." Lou produced both from the hand-warming pocket of her sweatshirt. "Go ahead."

Fen took a deep breath. "They officially ruled the fire as arson."

"Your source?"

He shook his head. "Can't say. It was told to me in confidence."

He could tell Lou didn't like it, but she knew this was part of the game. She huffed, but said, "What else?"

"Bailey will require skin grafts on the palm of her left hand. She tried to enter the back door of the trailer. It was like nothing else mattered."

Lou gave her head a double nod. "From what I could squeeze out of the hospital staff, that doesn't surprise me. What else?"

"Bailey will tell you she's not going back to school. I'm going to tell her she needs to, but I don't mean it. I want her to win a battle."

Lou allowed her pen to rest without making note of Fen's last statement. She stared at him. "It's true. You're a complicated man who plays complex games." She held her pen at the ready. "Anything else?"

"Have you done background research on Bailey?"

"Some. It's sketchy and not very pleasant. What have you found?"

"Nothing yet, but something in the trailer was important enough to Bailey that she sacrificed her hand to try to get it. I think it might have something to do with her father."

Lou rocked as she nodded. "He died in an off-shore accident on an oil rig. Bailey was seven."

Fen grunted that he understood.

"Wait a minute," said Lou. "You're giving me a story out of order. Start at the beginning and take me through until the time you left the hospital."

"I'll take you from the time I picked up Bailey in the morning until we pulled up on the fire. It's not the full story, but it'll give you a good idea of what happened."

She pointed her pen at him, and flames danced in her eyes. "I told you not to play games with me. I need the complete story."

"Calm down. If Thelma hears you raise your voice, she'll blame me and I'll have to listen to her complain for a solid week."

"Then tell me everything about the fire."

"I will. Half tonight and half tomorrow on the way to Houston. Bring your recorder."

Chapter Twenty

After an early start, Fen and Lou made good time in Lou's Camry hybrid as they headed south on Highway 6. Bryan and College Station were behind them; the small city of Navasota came into view. Fen shifted in his seat. "There's a cafe past the center of town that has excellent coffee and we can grab something for breakfast."

The fall morning had just enough bite in it that the coffee mugs doubled as hand-warmers. Instead of waiting for a table to open up in the noisy dining room, they ate alfresco. A picnic table on the back patio allowed them to enjoy a breakfast of ham, fried egg, and cheese on a buttery croissant in relative privacy. Rays of sunshine cut through the almost bare limbs of a gangly tree. The light seemed to dance in Lou's hair, and Fen became mesmerized.

"What are you staring at?"

He looked away, embarrassed, then brought his gaze back. "I was wondering what colors I'd have to mix to capture the way the sun is playing off your hair. Early morning light through trees makes getting out of bed to paint worthwhile."

She brought her hand to her hair and tucked one side behind an ear. "Sorry about looking like such a hag last night. I dressed down and scrubbed off the makeup so I could convince Thelma I didn't have designs on you. After seeing your portrait of Sally, I shouldn't have bothered. I understand why you still talk to her."

Instead of responding, Fen took a bite of his sandwich. It was a nice day, and he'd already had his early morning talk with his wife. Also, he and Lou had picked up where they left off on last night's discussion of the fire. Her lack of follow-up questions told him he'd done a decent job communicating details.

As Fen chewed, he mentally crossed his fingers for luck and hoped his plan to help Bailey would go smoothly. Lou must have read his thoughts. "Are you thinking about Bailey?"

"Yeah."

"Thought so. You have that concerned father look on your face."

This jarred him into a laugh, but Lou's raised eyebrows challenged him to deny it. He took the coward's way out. "I could use a refill of coffee. Would you mind getting it for me?"

She surprised him. "Nice try, but you don't really want or need any more coffee. We're headed for heavy traffic, and I don't know my way around Houston. Looking for a bathroom isn't my idea of a good use of time. There's a deadline to meet and you don't want to go anywhere near me if I miss it."

They finished their breakfast and were soon on their way. Fen was mentally rehearsing what he'd say to Bailey when Lou caught him by surprise. "Do you plan on telling me why your former father-in-law hates you so much?"

The bluntness of the question momentarily stunned Fen. "What have you heard?"

She shook her head. "There you go again, answering a question with a question."

Fen shrugged. "It's common knowledge around the county. We were close. He spent a lot of time and money helping me get elected as sheriff. All was good between us. We went through the heart transplant together. Me, Mr. Newman, and Lori prayed throughout the surgery. Everything went fine, and we thought we were in the clear. Everything was good for a long while, then her body started rejecting the new heart. Mr. Newman and I agreed that we'd press the doctors to put Sally back on the donor list."

Lou cast a quick gaze at him. "Did you do that without discussing it with Sally?"

"Yeah. It's a mistake I regret. It took a few months, but I came around to her way of thinking. The problem was, I had to tell her father that his eldest daughter didn't want another heart, and she'd decided on cremation. Sally told me she didn't want a grave and to scatter her ashes in the river. He's hated me ever since."

"Does he know you haven't followed her wishes concerning her ashes in the river?"

Fen turned his head to face her. "We're not exactly on speaking terms. Mr. Newman is a man who inherited some of the most productive land in the state. He's used to having things his way and thinks I should have made Sally get the second heart. He lost it when I honored Sally's desire to be cremated. In his way of thinking, funerals should only take place at a church or a funeral home. The only proper burial place is in a cemetery, and a slab of marble marks the grave."

"It sounds like he blames you for everything."

Fen shifted his gaze to a fallow field, and his thoughts wandered. The land had given up its crop and was resting, waiting for the next planting. Things would change. They always did. He spoke his next words without thinking. "It won't be long before Mr. Newman has someone to hate besides me."

"What was that?"

"Nothing. I need to come up with something to say to Bailey that won't make me sound like a worried father."

Words were sparse for the rest of the journey to the massive complex of hospitals near the heart of Houston. Lou focused on the onboard map display and the mechanical voice that told her where and when to turn. The car came to rest in a parking garage marked for visitors.

Lou went to the trunk and pulled out Fen's walker. "We should have brought a wheelchair."

Fen locked his knee brace. "I'll be fine."

It took twenty minutes of walking on hard floors to reach Bailey's room. Fen knocked. No answer. He tried again. Still no answer. After turning the knob, he eased the door open, but then backed away. "You go first."

Lou cocked her head. "Are you afraid?"

Fen didn't respond, but gave Lou a hard look and motioned for her to go in.

She did, and he followed. Bailey lay flat on her back with a cannula in her nose, leading to a supply of oxygen. Her eyes were open, but she made no move to acknowledge her visitors. Her right hand lay across her stomach, but she'd buried the left under a sheet and blanket.

While Fen and Lou stood at the foot of the bed, a nurse came in. "Look, Bailey. You have visitors."

Nothing moved on Bailey but the shallow fall and rise of her chest and the occasional blink of eyelids. The nurse moved to Bailey's side. "I'm going to raise your head so you can get a good look at these people. Can you tell me who they are?"

No response.

"Are they relatives? Friends?"

Instead of answering, Bailey simply shook her head to show they didn't fit under either category.

The nurse signaled for Fen and Lou to meet her in the hall.

Once there, Fen took as much weight off his bad leg as he could. "What's wrong with her? Can't she talk?"

"She can talk, scream, cuss, cry, and do all the other things a normal teenage girl can do. Her voice is still raspy, but she can spit fire when she wants to."

"Then why isn't she talking?" asked Lou.

"The doctor told her this morning she'd need another skin graft, and he couldn't promise she'd ever have full use of her left hand. Silence is part of the process of her coming to grips with that new reality."

The nurse cast her gaze up to meet his. "You must be Fen Maguire, the artist."

He nodded. "Did she tell you that?"

"She calls you Mr. Fen. A policeman from where you live came yesterday and tried to talk to her. She told him to pound sand. He gave me your name and the story of how you saved her. I looked you up on the internet. You lead an interesting life, Sheriff."

"Former sheriff."

Fen rubbed a palm across his cheek. "Do you think Bailey will speak to either of us today?"

"It won't hurt to try. The sooner she talks, the better it will be for her."

He turned to Lou. "I'll go first and stir her up a little. Her tongue works best when she's mad. I'm the vinegar, you can be the sugar."

The nurse chuckled. "You two make a good team."

Fen pushed his walker into the door, making a loud sound. He popped it down hard after each step until he stood by her bed. "I have a bone to pick with you, Bailey."

Her eyes fluttered.

"My knee is taking twice as long to heal because of you."

This earned a shifting of her eyes to look at his face, but no words.

"You're not the only one who had to go to the hospital. I coughed up so much smoke I thought I was a chimney."

She shifted her gaze away from him. He needed to get through to her.

"We both could have died. You might think life isn't worth living, but the next time you pull a stunt like that, don't count on me rescuing you."

Her voice came out weak and rough. "Leave me alone."

"No. I won't leave you alone until I've had my say and you apologize."

"Get used to waiting."

Now that her words flowed, he needed to get off his feet. He plopped down in the recliner by her bed. "If you don't want to apologize, then I'll need to charge you for all the supplies I bought you."

"I didn't start that stupid fire."

"Neither did I, but I suffered the financial loss."

Her voice rose to a higher pitch. "Are you kidding? I lost everything I owned."

He shrugged. "What? A few clothes from garage sales and discount stores."

Her face flushed. "Shut up. You don't know what I lost in that fire."

He pointed his index finger at her. "You can't count the bicycle. I think you stole it."

"I didn't steal it. I can show you the house that had it in a garage sale."

Fen flipped away the explanation. "It was the only thing that survived the fire, so you still can't count it. See? You lost nothing of real value in the fire."

"Yes, I did!" she shouted.

"Do you mean the portrait you painted of your father?"

Her eyes opened wider than he thought possible. Her voice squeaked out. "How did you know?"

He pulled himself up on his walker. "There's a lady coming in to talk to you. Her name is Lou. She's a newspaper reporter, and a very good one. She did research on you that showed your father died when you were seven." Fen pulled a photo from the inside pocket of his jacket. "Here's a copy of the picture that appeared in the paper when he died. You need to think about your next portrait of him and how you can improve on the one that burned."

A shaking right hand took the photo. Bailey blinked away tears as she stared. "It's the same photo I used last time."

Fen moved toward the door.

"Where are you going?"

"To get something to drink while you tell your story to Lou Cooper."

"But—"

"And drop the Mr. You're an adult now and adults call me Fen."

When he returned, he found Bailey and Lou chirping like they'd known each other all their lives. They exchanged conspiratorial looks with each other when asked what they'd discussed. He brought the visit to an end by saying, "Lou has a deadline to meet, so we need to get going. Have they given you any idea how long you'll be here?"

"At least a couple more days for inhalation therapy." She held up her left hand. "I don't know about this."

Fen reached into his pocket and pulled out a phone. He handed it to Bailey. "Keep me posted."

Disbelief and joy competed as she mumbled unintelligible words.

"A late birthday present," said Fen. "I noticed you didn't

have one, and I understand it's necessary for a senior in high school to stay in touch with friends."

She continued to stare at the screen that would give her access to the world. "This is the best thing ever, but we all know I'm not going back to school."

Fen pursed his lips together as he looked at Lou with an accusatory stare.

"Sorry," said Lou. "It slipped out after I told Bailey about her apartment and studio."

"That's the problem with reporters," said Fen. "They don't know when to stop reporting."

Lou handed Bailey a business card that included all the ways to contact her. "Like Fen said, stay in touch."

Fen and Lou made it to the elevator and waited for the doors to slide open. Fen asked, "Did you get your story?"

"Oh, yeah. I have enough for this week's lead and three or four follow-up stories. One will be a human-interest piece on Bailey that might stretch into weekly updates."

The doors parted and Lieutenant Creech took a step forward before coming to an abrupt halt halfway out of the elevator. He gathered himself and came further into the hallway. Fen and Lou both waited for him to speak.

"I'm glad I ran into you. Have you seen Bailey?"

Both nodded.

"How is she? I mean, is she talking today?"

"A little," said Fen.

"That's great. She wasn't ready yesterday. I still need to get a statement from her about the fire."

"Do you suspect her?" asked Lou.

Creech let out a laugh. "No chance of that." The lieutenant walked his fingers around the cowboy hat he held in his hands before focusing on Fen. "We might have gotten off to a rocky start, but I want to say how much I respect you. You did an awesome job as sheriff and now you're the hero of the county. I hope you'll forgive me for acting like a jerk." He extended a hand.

Fen took it and gave a firm handshake. "I'll share the blame with you."

Creech shifted his gaze to Lou. "Have you been to the office today?"

"No. We left at first light. What's going on?"

A smile spread across his face. "There's going to be a wedding. Lori Newman will soon be Sheriff Lori Creech."

Fen stuck out his hand again and pumped the lieutenant's for all it was worth. "Congratulations. You're getting a fine woman."

After more backslapping and well wishes, Fen and Lou took the elevator down. Once in her car, she said, "I wasn't expecting that from Lieutenant Creech."

Fen mumbled, "Looks like Mr. Newman is going to gain a son-in-law and lose another big chunk of land. That's not a good trade."

Chapter Twenty-One

Fen stood in the driveway watching Lou's car as it sped toward the front gate. Out of the corner of his eye, he noticed movement. This time Sam didn't catch him unaware. He kept watching as the front gate shut behind the Camry. "Anything going on I should know about?"

"I killed another wild hog last night and butchered it. Thought we'd take it to the family of that cop you call Ski."

"You don't like cops."

Neither Sam's words nor countenance showed the slightest hint of emotion. "Thelma says he's a good man."

"Have you had lunch?"

He nodded. "Fresh pig cooked over a campfire."

"Are you ready to go?"

Another nod. "I told Thelma we're going to town."

After Fen put the walker in the bed of his fire-scorched truck, he climbed into the passenger's side and fastened his seatbelt. Sam hated wearing a seatbelt and always waited until he was at the front gate to buckle up.

"You didn't ask about Bailey," said Fen.

"No need. Thelma talked with her."

"I thought you were busy butchering a hog."

Sam didn't reply. How the two communicated remained unsolved.

After delivering enough meat to sustain the family for some time to come, Sam started the truck. "Where to?"

Fen rubbed his chin. "Let's go back to Clete's trailer."

"Nothing left but ashes."

Fen turned his head. "I bet they didn't have a Choctaw Indian look through the ashes."

"Good point."

Except for two thick metal I-beams, axles, wheels, and scraps of tin, not much remained of the trailer. Sam used a stick to probe and found a cast-iron skillet and a Dutch oven. He put both in the back of the truck. The Dutch oven earned a nod of approval.

Fen intended to take Bailey's bicycle, but the heat from the fire melted the front tire, rim and spokes. He was ready to call off the search when Sam stood up straight and looked around. He locked his gaze on the backyard. "What is it, Sam?"

He pointed. "That's not right."

"It's a junk lawn mower. Leave it."

"Not that. The outhouse. It's too far from the trailer."

Fen hadn't noticed the distance before, but Sam was right. The outhouse was a good fifty yards from the back porch. It was worth a look, but not a walk on his sore leg. "You go," said Fen.

Sam shook his head. "Evil spirits live in those little wooden houses."

Fen huffed. "It's not spirits, but snakes you're afraid of."

"Both. You look."

With the leg brace locked, Fen moved the walker a step at a time toward the outhouse. From a distance, the structure looked several decades old. As he drew near, it became obvious he'd misjudged more than the age of the structure.

There was no door facing the trailer, so he walked around the building and saw a lock and hasp. As he studied the door, it dawned on him it had been hung with newer hinges mounted on the outside.

Fen hollered, "Bring me a screwdriver."

While Sam retrieved the tool, Fen inspected the construction of the building. Old barnwood and rusted tin had been used to give the outdoor privy the appearance of many decades of age. The sharp corners and straight lines revealed the building wasn't as old as it looked from a distance. Also, the dimensions were all wrong. It was much deeper than necessary.

Sam went to work with the screwdriver and soon had the barn-style hinges loose from the door frame. He pulled the door back enough to see inside, then let out a grunt and held the door away from the building for Fen to look.

The room was three times as deep as it was wide, an optical illusion from the back porch. Black garbage bags bulged from shelves as the odor of marijuana escaped the building. Another object on a shelf caught Fen's eye. He pushed the door back until the hasp with the lock securing it creaked. Turning sideways, he slid through the opening and took down a spiral notebook. His hand found the phone in his jacket pocket and he soon had photos of each page. He closed the notebook, put it back on a shelf and slid through the gap into fresh air.

"Put it back like we found it," said Fen. "We need to get out of here fast, and I need to make another stop before we go home."

Sam worked the screws back in place and soon they were rounding the mound of burned down debris that was once the home of Clete Brumbaugh.

The truck was in reverse when a horn sounded behind them. Sam checked the rearview mirror and said, "Trouble."

Fen turned his head to see who had blocked the driveway. It was his turn to moan. Fen stepped out of the truck and used its bed to steady himself.

He didn't have a chance to speak before he heard, "You're trespassing."

Fen regarded his former father-in-law. "I thought this trailer belonged to Clete Brumbaugh."

"He rented it from me and you're trespassing on my property."

"Actually, I'm not. I came to get his niece's bicycle, but it burned too."

Nathaniel Newman cast his gaze to the scorched grass in the front yard. "You came for a bicycle? Then that's what you'll leave with. Get it off my land."

Fen hollered, "Sam, get Bailey's bicycle and load it." He turned to Mr. Newman. "There's a cast-iron skillet and a Dutch oven we found. Sam wants to clean them up and use them. Do you want them?"

"I've got nothing against Sam, other than he works for a murderer. He can take them."

"That's mighty generous of you, since Clete's niece has more of a claim to them than either you or me."

Mr. Newman took a step toward Fen and lowered his voice. "A crew will be here tomorrow to dig a hole and bury everything that wasn't here a hundred years ago. They'll put up no trespassing signs, too. If I catch you on any of my properties, you'll either go to jail or the funeral home. It all depends on who catches you."

Fen wanted to give a warning of his own, but Mr. Newman had already turned to leave. That conversation would have to wait until the landowner was in a more receptive mood.

Once back in the truck, Sam wasted no time in leaving the property. "Where to?" he asked once they were on a county road.

"Chuck Forsythe's law office."

Sam nodded. "I'll stay in the truck. I don't like lawyers."

CANDY FORSYTHE LOOKED up from her computer screen as Fen hobbled in. She stood and with a jerk of her head, motioned for him to follow her. On the way to Chuck's office, she asked, "Coffee, tea, water, or just an ice pack?"

"Water and an ice pack, please."

Chuck rose from his desk as Fen entered, and Candy settled him on the sofa with a chair to elevate his leg. She disappeared as Chuck brought two chairs in tight. "You look a little better than when I saw you in the hospital, but not much."

"It's been a long day. This morning Lou Cooper and I went to Houston to see Bailey. Lou's writing the lead story for tomorrow's paper."

"Anything I should know about?"

"It's the same story you got from me in the hospital, except it's told from Bailey's perspective."

Candy came in with water, a dishtowel, and ice packs. She soon had the packs applied. "You've been on that leg too much."

Fen nodded in agreement. "I was telling Chuck about my trip to Houston this morning. Lou Cooper drove."

"Interesting," said Candy. She gave Chuck a look that Fen didn't know how to interpret. "You used to hate talking to the press."

"She had me over a barrel. She found out I have a P.I. license and threatened to print it. I had to barter with her."

The next question came from Chuck. "What's your read on Ms. Cooper?"

"She's smart. Smart enough to dress down and not wear makeup when she came to the house to get my version of the fire. She told Thelma it wouldn't be right if she ate in the formal dining room. We dined by the light of the fire pit."

"Wow. She is smart," said Candy. "I made the mistake of sitting in Sally's chair once and Thelma still gives me the stink eye."

"Lou also won Bailey over, which is saying something."

"How serious are the injuries?" asked Candy.

"Bad enough for two skin grafts."

"Such a shame."

"Yeah, but at least it won't affect her ability to paint. She'll have an apartment and a studio over the garage waiting for her when she gets out of the hospital."

Both Chuck and Candy gave nods of approval.

Fen moved on. "Are rumors of the big marriage going around yet?"

Chuck and Candy looked at each other and shook their heads. "What marriage?"

"Lieutenant Creech was coming off the hospital's elevator when Lou and I were leaving. He acted like we were the best of buddies, apologized, and said he and Lori Newman would soon tie the knot."

Candy leaned forward. "Did he say when?"

"Details should be in tomorrow's newspaper."

Chuck leaned back. "You've been busy."

The ice pack slipped off Fen's leg and Candy caught it before it hit the floor. While she replaced it, Fen looked at Chuck. "Now it's your turn to get busy. Sam and I went to the trailer today to look for something that would tell us why somebody torched it."

Chuck kept a poker face, but asked, "I thought Danni Worth scoured the crime scene with a fine-tooth comb."

"She did, but they didn't look far enough in the back yard." Fen told them about the outhouse and its contents.

After he listened with eyes closed and hands folded in his lap, Chuck asked, "How do you want to proceed?"

"I want you to call Tom Stevens and tell him to get the contents of the outhouse tonight. Don't tell him I gave you the information and be sure he understands he's not to include Lori or anyone from the sheriff's department in this. It needs to be state troopers only."

Chuck tilted his head. "You're serious about not wanting to be sheriff again, aren't you?"

"Too many memories. Tom will clean up the sheriff's department when he takes over, so I need to keep my name from appearing in the newspaper and out of any official reports."

"From what you've said about Lou Cooper, that may be difficult."

Fen couldn't help but grin. "I enjoy a challenge."

Chuck shifted in his chair as if he thought the meeting had ended.

"One more thing," said Fen. "I had a brief, unpleasant chat with Nathaniel Newman this afternoon."

Chuck leaned back. "This has been an eventful day."

"He blocked us in when Sam and I were leaving with what we could salvage from the trailer. He told me I was trespassing and threatened to have me arrested."

"I'm surprised he didn't shoot you."

"We discussed it."

Candy chimed in. "I checked the property records. He owns the land."

"And tomorrow he's going to bury all evidence of the fire.

They may bury the outhouse along with what remains of the trailer."

Fen pulled out his phone. "I took photos of pages from a notebook I found in the outhouse. It looks like a ledger of some sort, but I can't make sense of it."

Fen pulled up the first photo and showed it to Chuck. He took a quick look and said, "Don't look at me. Candy's the one who likes to work puzzles."

She took the phone from Fen, manipulated it until she'd sent herself an email and handed it back. "I'll see if I can make heads or tails out of this."

Chuck said, "Don't send this to anyone if you want to stay under the radar. In fact, it would be best if you delete the photos after Tom picks up the drugs and the notebook tonight."

Fen snapped his fingers. "I need to tell you something that slipped my mind. The pistol that killed Clete– I know for a fact that Lori gave it back to her father. He carried it in his truck."

Chuck raised his eyebrows. "Evidence is stacking up against Mr. Newman."

"Speaking of the devil," said Fen. "I'd like for you to arrange a meeting between me and him with you and his attorney present."

"And the purpose of the meeting?"

"An attempt at partial reconciliation. I want to propose we bury Sally's ashes in a grave on the property line that divides his land from mine."

Candy stood. "You *do* like a challenge."

Chapter Twenty-Two

After eight days of rest, Fen was ambulatory again and had put the walker back in the garage. He answered the knock on the front door at 6:00 p.m. Lou looked down at his leg. "No walker, and no brace. I'm impressed. Where's Bailey?"

"In her apartment. She'll be down in a little while. I'm glad you brought a wool scarf; it's going to be nippy on the patio."

"How does she like her new home?"

"Go ask her." He pointed down a hallway. "If you don't remember, go out that door and take the stairway to the left."

She spun on the soles of brown boots as he added, "It looks a little different now. Take photos if you like."

"I planned on it."

Fen checked with Thelma on when to expect supper. Her reply was typical. "You'll eat when it's ready. I already put something for you to graze on out there, so get out of my kitchen and let me finish. I swear, between you and Sam it's a wonder my hair isn't white as snow."

Fen beat a hasty retreat to the back porch and stood by the fire pit with hands extended toward the flames. He moved to a charcuterie board and piled paper-thin salami and a slice of camembert cheese on a cracker. After nodding his approval, he had two more.

Bailey and Lou made their appearance, which saved him from a fourth helping. "Why are we eating out here?" asked Bailey.

"That's my fault," said Lou. "I wanted to make sure Thelma didn't think I wanted to become the woman of the house, so I talked myself out of ever sitting at the dining room table."

"Huh?"

Fen dismissed any desire to explain with a wave of his hand and a quick, "I'll tell you about it some other time. There's chips and spicy cheese dip or meat, crackers, and cheeses if you need a snack."

"Yum," said Bailey. "Real food and not what they served in the hospital."

"Tell me about your last surgery," said Lou.

"It hurt. Not during, but after. They took skin from the inside of my thigh and grafted it on my hand and fingers." She held up a bulky bandage. "The doctor said if there are no complications, I won't need another skin graft. I still haven't looked at it and I'm not going to until all the bandages are off."

Thelma stepped out the door and stood with hands on hips. "Miss Bailey, what are you doing standing there? You sit down and let Mr. Fen or Miss Lou get you something to eat. My Lord, what's wrong with you two? Can't you see this child needs to sit?" She huffed something else under her breath then spoke in her normal, loud voice. "I'll be out with your food in five minutes."

Once the door slammed shut behind Thelma, Fen turned to Lou. "I knew she liked you, but that proved it. To receive correction from Thelma means she has you on speed dial. How much information has she funneled your way?"

"I never reveal my sources."

Lou put chips and dip on Bailey's plate and handed it to her. She balanced it on her legs, took a bite, and spoke around it. "I read your stories about the fire. They were very good."

"Thanks to you and Fen, I had plenty to work with."

Bailey crammed in another bite and had to wait until she chewed and swallowed before she could continue. "Not just those stories, but the others, too. It sounds like Mr. Newman is the prime suspect for the fire and Uncle Clete's murder."

Lou settled in the chair next to Bailey after taking a throw from the back of her chair and placing it over the teen's shoulders. "Several sources came forward with good information."

"Like what?"

"Like Mr. Newman had all traces of the trailer buried even though Danni Worth hadn't released the crime scene. It's also rumored that Sheriff Lori told her father to clear the land to hide evidence." Lou leaned back in her chair. "I didn't put that in my article because I only had one source."

Fen considered having another cracker with cheese, but decided against it. "What else is convincing you that Mr. Newman is involved?"

"He owned the land and the trailer."

Bailey interrupted with her mouth full. "That trailer was a dump."

"That much I can verify," said Fen.

Lou allowed Bailey to chew and swallow before adding, "And Mr. Newman refused to provide me with proof that Clete paid to live there."

"Uncle Clete told me it was empty when he moved in and Mr. Newman let him live there because he didn't want to shell out the money it would cost to move it."

Lou's eyebrows came together. "My sources told me a different story."

Fen took a seat so he could see both women and directed his gaze at Lou. "What's the different story?"

"That Mr. Newman agreed to let Clete live for free if he'd get a percentage of the profits from Clete's sale of marijuana."

Fen shifted his gaze to Bailey. "Does that sound plausible?"

"I'd believe that over the story about not wanting to move the trailer. Uncle Clete said Mr. Newman is a bitter old man who thought of nothing but hurting you and making more money. It's hard for me to believe he didn't know about the marijuana growing on his property. I found it the first week I was there."

Fen's gaze went back to Lou. "Any other rumors floating around?"

Lou lifted her chin. "We in the press like to call them unsubstantiated tips. Another one I received was from a man who told me the accident that injured Deputy Salinski wasn't an accident. He said they hauled the patrol car from the site of the crash to the impound yard and now it's gone."

"That's a serious accusation," said Fen.

Lou nodded in agreement. "It's not there. I checked."

Fen moved to the edge of his seat. "Are you sure?"

"The tow truck driver I spoke to said he took it to the impound yard. Now, no one at the sheriff's office knows where it went."

"Someone knows," said Fen. "My guess is they don't want to take the time to look into it, which doesn't surprise me. You haven't exactly endeared yourself to that department."

"True," said Lou. "Lori and Lieutenant Creech are too busy planning their wedding and honeymoon to get back with me."

Bailey shook her head. "Why would anyone want to get married two days before Christmas?"

Lou shivered, but Fen didn't think it was from the cold. He looked through the window and saw Thelma coming with food. "Perhaps Lt. Creech isn't good at remembering dates, and getting married at Christmas would make it hard to forget an anniversary."

The meal progressed with little conversation. Thelma had cut Bailey's steak into bite-size pieces before serving her. Dessert was chocolate lava cake served in individual ramekins.

It didn't take long for fatigue and a mild food coma to overtake Bailey. "Everything was so good. I'm going to take a pill and try out that new queen-size bed."

"Sleep well," said Lou. Fen nodded a good night.

After the door shut, Lou took in a deep breath and let it out with a sigh that sounded like contentment. "She's adjusting well."

Fen raised his eyebrows in doubt. "She's only been here two days. If you do a follow-up story in a few months, I bet she won't think everything is so perfect."

Lou tilted her head. "I didn't have you pegged as a pessimist."

"More like a realist. I had a lot of dealings with young men and women her age when I wore a badge. Their decision-making ability left a lot of room for improvement."

"No one twisted your arm to take her in."

Fen grinned. "I like the occasional challenge."

Thelma came out with an insulated carafe of decaf coffee and two mugs. "If you want more, you'll have to make it yourself. The kitchen is closed."

They both thanked Thelma again as she walked past the fire pit on the way to her small home. She turned. "I told Miss Bailey to call me if she needs anything in the night. Don't you go peekin' in on her, Mr. Fen. You'll scare that poor child to death with those ratty pajamas you wear."

Lou waited until Thelma was out of sight. "The reporter in me senses there's a story in what she said." A mischievous smile revealed a line of white teeth. "Tell me about your ratty pajamas."

"Nothing to tell," said Fen. "I threw them away two days ago. We don't have many secrets around here, but I don't leave my bedroom unless I'm fully dressed." He took a breath. "Speaking of your next story, what's it going to be?"

Lou chuckled. "I can take a hint. Your choice of sleepwear isn't up for discussion. My next article will focus on a gas can found in the driveway of Clete Brumbaugh's trailer after the fire. Two reliable sources say the can is red and that Mr. Newman kept it in the bed of his truck."

"He did like to make small brush piles and burn them." Fen rubbed his knee. "How much did it hold?"

"Two gallons."

"Yeah, it could have been Mr. Newman's. He used to carry a can like that."

Lou widened her eyes just a little and nodded in satisfaction. "Newman Ranch is written on it in black marker."

"Have you seen the can?"

"Only a photo. It's supposed to be in evidence at the sheriff's department. I interviewed Danni Worth after I received the photos. She was tightlipped, but I could tell it surprised her that I learned about it. She wouldn't comment on it being part of the inventory. Neither would anyone at the sheriff's office."

Fen stood and walked a few steps into the night before turning around. "Someone could have taken it from Mr. Newman's truck."

"True, but he or someone he hired could also have left it there after they started the fire."

"Does the photo show anything else?"

"It's a close up so it doesn't show smoke or flames, only the can. Do you remember seeing it when you parked in the driveway?"

Fen wagged his head. "I was focused on getting to Bailey. I don't recall anything in the driveway."

A comfortable silence fell over the patio as the temperature ticked down. Lou put down her empty coffee cup and shoved her hands in the pockets of her coat. "Anything else you'd like to tell me?"

He chuckled. "Don't you mean, is there anything else I'd like to read about in the local newspaper?"

"What about something off the record?"

"All right. I'm not sure you'll consider what I have to say newsworthy, but I don't want it to be common knowledge until I say you can run with it."

Lou moved to the edge of her seat and took out her notebook. "It won't go to print unless I have it verified by two other sources."

Fen shook his head. "That's not good enough. Forget I mentioned it."

"If you think you can keep a secret in this county, you're mistaken. I know you have a meeting scheduled tomorrow with Nathaniel Newman. You might as well tell me what it's about."

Fen issued an unconvincing yawn. "I hope you enjoyed the meal, and you got something useful from your talk with Bailey."

Lou stood. "Thank you for the meal and warm hospitality. It's a shame it cooled off so fast out here. Don't bother showing me out."

Chapter Twenty Three

Fen walked through the doorway of Chuck Forsythe's law office at 10:15 a.m., a full fifteen minutes before Nathaniel Newman and his attorney were scheduled to arrive. Candy met him with her usual smile. "How's Bailey adjusting?"

"Hard to tell. She seemed alright last night, but I didn't see her this morning. I need to speak with Thelma and tell her not to baby Bailey so much. She set a dangerous precedent this morning by serving breakfast in bed."

Candy shooed away the idea with a flip of her wrist. "From what I know of Bailey, she won't tolerate someone hovering over her, and we all know how Thelma is. Special treatment will soon end by mutual agreement."

"Good. I wasn't looking forward to that conversation."

Candy looked at the clock on the wall opposite her desk. "Chuck's expecting you. Go on back. I'll let you know when your guests arrive."

Even though the door was open, Fen knocked on the door frame. Chuck looked up from a stack of papers on his desk and waved him in. "I'm going over this proposal you want me to deliver to Mr. Newman and his attorney. I beefed it up with a bunch of legal-speak, but the meaning is the same."

Fen walked across the spacious office and sat in the first of two leather chairs in front of Chuck's desk. "I don't know about you, but I'm surprised Mr. Newman agreed to meet at all, let alone in your office."

"He must have something up his sleeve besides his arm. I wouldn't put it past that cagey old man to have an ambush planned for you."

"I'll be disappointed if he doesn't."

Both men traded smiles, but Chuck's didn't last long. "I know you've thought about this for a long time, but once you both agree to it, there's no going back. You'll never be able to honor Sally's wish."

Fen dipped his head. "I've turned this over in my mind a thousand times. I think Sally would want me to reconcile with her father more than anything."

"What if he refuses?"

"I expect him to at least once. Then I'll sweeten the offer."

"You didn't tell me about that. What do you have in mind?"

Chuck's phone rang. He listened and said, "Put them in the conference room and offer something to drink." He looked at Fen. "We'll discuss your second offer later. Who knows, Mr. Newman may be reasonable today."

The attorney picked up a file folder and stood. "How's Bailey?"

"Frustrated. She wants to jump in and paint, but the doctor's instructions are for her to be extra careful with the skin grafts and not overdo it. She agreed to paint for only twenty minutes at a time."

Chuck placed a hand on Fen's shoulder. "Teenage girls

have a unique concept of time. Fifteen minutes means a full hour, if it's something they like to do."

"That's the same thing her doctor said and why he told her she could only paint for twenty minutes before she rested an hour. After translation, it means he wants her painting restricted to an hour, followed by twenty minutes of rest in bed or on the couch."

Chuck led the way down the hall to a room with a table that sat ten comfortably and twelve if needed. Candy had already placed Mr. Newman and a man with salt and pepper hair on one of the long sides of the table. Mr. Newman wore his normal attire of jeans, boots, a cowboy cut shirt and sports coat. His attorney, Mr. Rosenthal, wore a tailored gray suit, a crisp white shirt with French cuffs, gold cufflinks, and a Rolex watch.

The two attorneys faced each other across the table, as did Fen and his former father-in-law. Candy sat at the far end of the table with a memo pad and pen at the ready. Chuck led things off by handing each man a copy of a document. "Take your time in reading this. If you need to confer alone, we'll step out of the room."

Both men read in silence. Mr. Newman pushed the two-page document away from him as if it might carry an infectious disease. He leaned into his attorney and delivered a salty response in a loud whisper.

Mr. Rosenthal nodded. "My client has no intention of agreeing to this."

Fen spoke up. "Perhaps your client doesn't realize I'm willing to compromise a promise to my late wife. This is my attempt to reconcile our differences."

Blood rushed to Mr. Newman's face. "You killed Sally, and I'd rather shake hands with the devil than have any dealings with you."

Mr. Rosenthal put his hand on Mr. Newman's forearm.

"What my client means is, if you are serious about any sort of reconciliation, it must start with you returning the land he gave to his daughter."

It was Chuck's turn. "That land is a gift to both husband and wife, and her death makes Mr. Maguire the sole owner of all four thousand acres."

Mr. Newman narrowed his eyes and spoke through clenched teeth. "I hope you're ready for a long, expensive court battle."

Chuck kept his usual calm demeanor, and Fen allowed him to do the talking. "Judge Rainey made it clear that my client is the sole owner. Let's move on."

Fen placed his palms flat on the table. "I would have thought the idea of burying Sally's ashes on the land next to your client's property would be acceptable. In fact, I'm willing to offer Mr. Newman his choice of headstones, provided he doesn't besmirch my good name by having something inappropriate engraved on it."

Mr. Newman's knuckles turned white. "What good name? You watched my daughter suffer and die when you could have insisted we find another heart. And then you desecrated her body by burning my Sally in fire like that of hell." He narrowed his eyes at Fen. "And that's the reward that awaits you. But first, you're going to suffer here on earth." He turned to his attorney. "Tell them."

Mr. Rosenthal complied. "As for your offer to designate a burial site along the property line, my client rejects your proposal outright. In addition, we will soon serve you with a civil lawsuit challenging Mr. Maguire's ownership of the land. Since you'll find out the details soon enough, there's no need to delay. My firm's first request will be for a change of venue, because of Mr. Maguire's past business relationships and friendship with Judge Rawlings. I have already made the supervising judge aware that my client can't expect to receive a fair trial in this county."

Fen expected this, and he believed Chuck did too. Neither reacted, which seemed to anger Mr. Newman all the more.

"Furthermore," said Mr. Rosenthal, "My client is prepared to file criminal complaints against Mr. Maguire for trespassing and harassment."

Chuck laughed out loud. "I hope you told your client the definition of harassment, and that I can line up witnesses twenty deep that will testify against him when I bring counter charges."

"You're just a hick lawyer," said Mr. Newman. "What do you know about harassment?"

Chuck didn't miss a beat. "As far as the threat to file a trespass charge, the land wasn't posted. Also, my client had permission to be on the property from Ms. Bailey Madison, the daughter of Cletus Brumbaugh's sister, who lived in the trailer until the fire made the trailer uninhabitable. You remember Mr. Brumbaugh. He occupied *your* trailer on land *you* own, Mr. Newman. He was shot with a pistol registered to *your* daughter, which multiple witnesses say *you* carried in your truck. His body washed downstream from *your* property. Shall I go on?"

Mr. Newman snapped a reply as he pointed at Fen, "They found Clete's body on his property."

Chuck gave a brief smile. "We're making progress, Mr. Newman. You admit that the property belongs to my client. Thank you for releasing your claim on it."

"He did no such thing," said Mr. Rosenthal.

With a tilt of his head, Chuck looked at the other attorney. "I hope your client has your number memorized. With all the publicity he's received in the past few weeks, I have a feeling he'll need you sooner than you think."

"Not with my daughter as sheriff."

Chuck's smile widened. "Thank you again, Mr. Newman. That last quote will make an excellent headline in the local paper."

"You wouldn't dare," said Mr. Rosenthal.

"Of course not. I'm an officer of the court and I don't divulge what's said in my office to the press." He pointed at both Candy and Fen. "But I can't speak for these two."

"I'll see you in court, counselor." Mr. Rosenthal rose and motioned for Mr. Newman to do the same.

"Don't bet on this going to court," said Fen.

The swarthy attorney issued a smile that pulled up the right half of his top lip. "And my promise to see you before a judge and jury goes double for you, Mr. Maguire. I'll take extra pleasure in litigating these cases."

Candy walked the two men out of the conference room and returned a short time later. "That was fun. Did you accomplish what you wanted, Fen?"

"I think so. I wanted to know if his hatred of me is keeping him blind to what's about to happen to him."

Chuck laced his fingers together in front of him. "Let's look at all the evidence against him."

Fen started off. "Newman land surrounds the boat ramp on all sides. Danni Worth believes Clete went in the river at or near the boat ramp. It seems likely that the murder took place there or on Newman property."

Candy took her turn. "The gun that killed Clete belonged to Lori, but we know she gave it to her father."

It was Fen's turn again. "Clete was growing marijuana on Newman land and had a modified outhouse full of it." Fen paused. "That reminds me. Did Tom Stevens turn over that log book to the brains in Austin?"

"He did, but there's no word back yet. It must be one heck of an encryption."

"Or something so simple it takes a child to figure it out," said Candy.

"I'll take another look at it," said Fen. He tilted his head. "Do either of you know anything about a gasoline can belonging to Mr. Newman found at the trailer fire?"

Candy shook her head while Chuck asked, "Where's the can now?"

"My source at the local paper told me it's supposed to be in evidence at the sheriff's office. I need to check with Danni Worth and see if she logged it into her evidence folder and turned it in to Lieutenant Creech."

"Not Lieutenant Creech for long," said Candy. "The story I heard is he's resigning and Lori will hire him as a consultant."

Fen's mouth hinged open for a few seconds. He closed it and said, "It's all making sense. Lori will be the sheriff, but Jake Creech will run the sheriff's department behind the scenes. But where does that leave us with Mr. Newman?"

"He's looking guilty to me," said Chuck. "They can win the individual charges against him, but not when they're stacked together. As the circumstantial and real evidence mounts up, a jury won't be able to ignore it. There's the gun, the marijuana patch on Mr. Newman's land, the drugs found in Mr. Newman's truck after the anonymous tip, the gas can, and the fire to destroy evidence."

Fen spoke before Chuck could go on. "I also heard there's a missing patrol car. It's the one Deputy Salinski almost died in when he chased a suspected drug dealer."

"Are you sure it's missing?" asked Chuck.

"It's not in the impound yard. I drove by there on my way here. I called a deputy I can trust, and he told me they stripped it of anything useful and sold it as scrap. He said that's what's happening with vehicles that aren't claimed in a timely manner."

Chuck allowed his thoughts to slip out as words. "Someone at the sheriff's office is running a chop shop."

Fen added, "If that's true, there's two sets of books. One for parts and one for the scrap."

"Doesn't surprise me," said Candy. "Shady things are going on in this county that never have before."

Fen turned to Chuck. "How long before Tom Stevens arrests Mr. Newman?"

"He'll be a lot closer after he learns about the gas can. He's keeping the Texas Rangers informed."

"Tell him to hold off as long as he can. I'm close to wrapping this thing up. Just one or two more pieces of hard evidence and the lid is going to blow off this county."

"What's your next step?" asked Chuck.

"I need to crack the code in Clete's book."

Chapter Twenty-Four

Fen arrived home with his thoughts running at a full gallop. He needed to spend however much time it took to make sense of the pages from the ledger he'd found in the outhouse. Hard copies of the photos waited for him in his office, but his growling stomach told him he needed to slow down and have lunch. Not only did he find Thelma in the kitchen, but also Bailey. His new tenant wore baggy, gray workout pants and a dark T-shirt, already stained with several colors of paint.

"What's for lunch?" asked Fen.

Thelma rose from a chair at the breakfast nook. "If you want something hot, I'll need to heat leftovers. If you're in a hurry, I can slap together a sandwich for you."

"Start slapping."

Fen took his seat across the table from Bailey. She had her head buried in the catalog of painting supplies. Without looking up, she said, "There's some cool stuff in here."

"Pick out what you like."

"Anything?"

"I retain the right to veto all requests."

She looked up. "They don't make what I really need."

"What's that?"

"A hand that doesn't look like a cheese pizza."

Fen closed his eyes for a full three seconds and wondered how to respond. He considered a flippant remark and rejected it. Perhaps he should tell her to buck up and be thankful to be alive. Neither sounded right, so he replied with silence.

Bailey shifted her gaze back to the catalog. "I'm used to holding a wooden painter's palate with a thumb hole. My preference is to work for hours without a break. All this laying down is drying out my paint."

"That's an easy enough fix," said Fen. "Have you found the wet palettes with the air tight lids in that catalog yet?"

"Huh?"

"Keep looking. They're about two-thirds of the way through."

Bailey flipped pages and then stopped. "Do these things work?"

"They're great for acrylics. They lay flat on a table and have a resealable lid. There's a thin sponge that you get damp and put on the bottom tray. Then, special paper goes on top of the sponge and you mix your paint on disposable sheets. If you need to take a break, you snap on the lid and the paint's ready to use when you start again."

"How cool! Can I get one?"

"Sure. It will save money on paint in the long run."

Bailey continued to read the details of the product.

As Thelma delivered Fen's sandwich with a wedge of pickle and chips, Bailey looked up. "There's another problem I'm having. My palette isn't at the right height. I have to twist and bend over every time I need to load my brush."

"Another easy fix. While I was healing from getting shot,

Sally got me one of those adjustable tables like you used in the hospital."

"The one that goes up and down and can roll anywhere you need?"

"It's in the garage. I'll bring it up for you."

Thelma drew back from the refrigerator. "No, you won't. That thing's awkward, heavy, and needs cleaning. I'll scrub it and get Sam to tote it up those stairs."

Bailey kept her finger in the catalog, closed it to look at the cover, and exclaimed, "This thing's over two years old."

"So?" said Fen. "The prices have changed, but most of the products are still available. I'll go online and order what you need this afternoon."

"I guess keeping old catalogs around is helpful from time to time."

Something clicked in Fen's mind, and he slowed his chewing. It wasn't a full-blown revelation, only a passing shadow of something his brain told him was important. He tried to grasp it, but it was like grabbing quicksilver with oily hands. He rose and picked up his plate and glass of iced tea.

Still trying to focus on the illusive wisp of a thought, he took a step toward the door. "I'll be in my office the rest of the day."

"Are you all right, Mr. Fen?" asked Bailey.

He kept walking and barely heard Thelma's fading voice. "He's fine, Miss Bailey. In one of his thinking moods."

Fen closed the door to his office and moved to the high-back leather chair behind his desk. Unscrambling the words in Clete Brumbaugh's code book called for a work station. Maybe later he'd move to the wing back chair where he talked with Sally. Right now, he needed to solve this puzzle.

"Clear your mind of all assumptions," Fen said to himself out loud. "Take a deep breath and let it out slow." He breathed deep three more times and experienced the calm that comes through practicing relaxation.

The blast of the doorbell interrupted the peace of the room. Thelma passed the office, mumbling and grumbling as she went to answer the front door. In less than a minute, he heard Thelma's crisp rap on the door. "Mr. Fen, Miss Danni wants to talk to you. I told her you're busy, but she said it's important."

Fen rose and walked around the desk. "Show her in."

Danni entered, and Thelma closed the door behind her. "That's an intimidating gatekeeper you have."

"I'd hate to tangle with her," said Fen.

"Did I interrupt anything?" She looked at his plate on the desk. "That was a dumb question. You're eating lunch."

Fen waved away the comment. "If I eat it, I'll get sleepy. If I don't, my stomach will launch a protest."

He continued before she could speak. "I'm glad you stopped by."

She smiled and put her hand on his arm. "Oh?"

Fen cleared his throat and turned toward the desk. "Have a seat. I heard a rumor today. I wonder if you can clear up something having to do with the fire at the trailer."

"I'll answer if I can."

"Did you log a gas can belonging to Mr. Newman on your inventory of items not destroyed by the fire?"

"I start by taking photographs of a crime scene and write a log of everything that looks important. After I blow up the photos on my computer, there's always something else to add to the list. It's amazing how many more things you find in a photo."

"Did you see a two-gallon gas can in the driveway?"

She nodded. "It was hard to miss. I'm surprised the fumes didn't ignite and turn it into a small bomb."

"I heard it belonged to Nathaniel Newman."

Danni gave her head a single nod. "I turned it over to Lieutenant Creech after I dusted it for prints and logged it."

"Did you get any prints off it?"

"Unfortunately, no. It was pretty well scorched. If the writing hadn't been on the side facing the road, we wouldn't know who it belonged to."

Fen shook his head. "Mr. Newman must be slipping. The man I knew wouldn't leave anything behind."

Danni dipped her head and brought it back up. "The reason I stopped by was to tell you the Texas Rangers are about an inch away from arresting Mr. Newman. I thought you'd like to know."

"I'm surprised they've waited this long."

"They're having trouble getting the gas can from Sheriff Lori."

Fen shook his head several times. "That's a fool's game she's playing."

"Do you think they'll arrest her along with her father?"

He looked past Danni to a row of books on a shelf. "It takes more than a misplaced gasoline can to get a sheriff arrested. If she can't find it soon, they'll go after Lieutenant Creech. I'm guessing he knows where it is and he's trying to protect his future father-in-law."

Danni swiveled in the chair to face the bookcase. "What are you looking at over my shoulder?"

Fen chuckled. "That book you pointed out to me the last time you were here. I was wondering how many college professors add a brief chapter to a previous publication, call it a second edition and double the price."

She rose and took down Fen's copy, flipped through it, and put it back. "Everything looks the same except the introduction and the last two chapters."

"What edition do you have?" asked Fen.

"Third."

"I have the original."

"That's because I didn't finish college until ten years after you did."

"Don't remind me of my age," said Fen, as he rose from his chair.

They walked to the front door, and Fen followed her down the steps to her van. "Thanks for the heads up on the arrest."

She looked at him and shielded her eyes with her hand from the bright sunlight. "I still don't see how a bloodhound like you stayed away from investigating this case."

He raised his eyebrows. "Are you sure I didn't?"

"I'd have read about it in the newspaper. Not much goes on in this county that Lou Cooper doesn't know about. The only thing she hasn't reported on is your relationship with her."

"Are you jealous?"

"What if I am?"

"Then you and Lou should start a lonely-hearts club. I'm not on the market."

Danni got in her car and waved goodbye as she eased down the driveway.

Fen made it back to his office and shut the door. He wanted to get his mind off Danni's flirting and her subtle accusation of something going on between him and Lou. He spent the next thirty minutes reviewing the book on photographing crime scenes. He then returned to his desk to work on the coded pages of the ledger. Two hours later, he lifted his head with a smile of satisfaction. He had the answer to the elusive code. All he needed to do was double check and contact Chuck Forsythe who'd notify the right people.

His cell phone vibrated. Verification would have to wait. He looked at the caller I.D. and swiped the green icon. "Hello, Lou."

"I'm mad."

The brief introduction left Fen wordless for a second. He recovered quickly. "You were mad when you left last night. Is it the same mad?"

"No. Well, sort of. You met with Mr. Newman and his hotshot attorney from College Station this morning. What did you discuss?"

"I tried to reconcile with Mr. Newman."

Lou let out a sarcastic huff. "Sure you did. Then you sang 'Kumbaya' while eating s'mores by a campfire. Come on, Fen, don't pull my leg."

"It's true. I offered to bury Sally's remains in a grave on the fence line that divides our properties. He turned me down flat."

"Even if that's true, you knew his answer before you asked. What was the meeting really about?"

"Off the record?"

"No, it's not off the record! This is how I make my living, and it's not by writing a sappy story about two silly men. You want to bury the proverbial hatchet and he wants a real one in your back."

Fen couldn't help but laugh. "Don't give him any ideas."

"When will Mr. Newman's arrest take place?"

"How should I know?"

"Has anyone ever told you how aggravating you are?"

Fen didn't reply, which caused Lou to let out a scream. "I'm pulling out my hair. Happy now?"

"Not particularly, but I have some advice for you."

"What's that?"

"Don't print the story on all the evidence against Mr. Newman."

Another scream and the call disconnected.

Fen returned to the task he was completing before Lou

interrupted him. After making his last notes, he dialed Chuck Forsythe and whispered, "There's no turning back now."

Chuck almost never answered his phone, but today he did. Fen asked, "Is Candy with you?"

"Yeah."

"Put it on speaker."

He heard the phone make a single click. Then, Chuck said, "You sound excited. Did you solve everything?"

"I figured out the code for the ledger. Call Tom Stevens and have him tell the Rangers to hold off on the arrest of Mr. Newman. I want Tom to get credit for everything. He'll make a very good sheriff."

"That job is yours for the taking," said Candy.

"No thanks. I don't mind wrapping everything up, but that badge will go to someone else." He took a breath. "I need you two and Tom to arrange a meeting with everyone that needs to be there. I'll disappear after the meeting."

"Two questions," said Chuck. "When do you want to bring everyone together, and is Lori going to jail?"

"Tomorrow afternoon, and as for Lori... I guess we'll see. Now, let me tell you how the code works and who all needs to be there."

Candy's voice came through loud and clear. "I'm ready with paper and pen."

Chapter Twenty-Five

The early morning routine went on as usual. Fen brought a cup of coffee to his office, took down the urn containing Sally's ashes, and told his wife his plans for the day. He then went to his studio and continued work on the painting he'd started the day Clete Brumbaugh's lifeless body drifted down the Brazos and lodged in a tree. The landscape didn't include the corpse.

He was still blending colors on his palette when Sam appeared by his side. If Fen hadn't seen Sam's reflection in the window when he silently entered the room, he might have twisted his knee again. Instead, he focused on making sure the color of a small bush was to his liking.

"Is there something I need to know about?" asked Fen in an even voice.

"How long do you want me to keep recordings from the cameras I put in all the vehicles?"

Fen turned to face him. "I forget to turn them on. What about you?"

"I don't trust cops. If the truck is running, I flip the switch."

"Have the cops bothered you anymore?"

Sam shook his head.

"If there's nothing of interest, delete the footage."

"What about the fire?"

Fen spun to fully face Sam. "Are you talking about the trailer fire?"

Sam nodded.

"There's footage of the fire at Clete's trailer?"

"You should know. You turned on the camera when you saw the flames and smoke."

Fen lowered his chin. "Bailey was driving. She must have turned it on and didn't tell me. Do you have the recordings?"

"Look on your phone," said Sam. "Don't you remember installing the app so you could view them?"

Fen slapped his forehead. His gaze shifted to his painting, but he was thinking about the fire. "I've been carrying around evidence in my pocket that clears an innocent man and didn't realize it."

When Fen turned to cast his gaze on Sam again, he was gone. He jerked his phone from his pocket, found the app, and located the video. After watching it on the small screen, he transferred the file to his email address. He went to his office and watched it three more times before forwarding it to Chuck with a note of explanation. It wasn't long before his phone rang.

"Where did you get this?" asked Chuck.

"I rigged all our vehicles with cameras. Bailey must have turned them on while I slept on the way back from the washed-out Halloween Carnival."

"This seals the deal," said Chuck. "How do you want Tom to handle Mr. Newman?"

"Have Tom detain him for questioning and bring him to the meeting." Fen paused. "By the way, where did you and Tom decide to have the meeting and when?"

"Here at my practice. In the conference room at one thirty. There's a big screen television."

Candy's voice came next. "You should know that the paper ran a special edition this morning. She lays out a convincing case against Mr. Newman."

Fen let out a huff of frustration. "I warned her, and now it's too late. She can't unprint the story."

Candy met Fen at the front door of the office. "Where did you park?" she asked.

"Three blocks over in front of the barbershop."

"Good. I almost called you to suggest the donut shop, but the barbershop is just as good."

Fen looked around. "Are you and Chuck the only ones here?"

"I sent my assistant to College Station to get printer cartridges. She didn't need to be here for what's going to happen."

Candy pointed to the door leading to the hallway. "Chuck's waiting for you in his office."

As usual, Chuck sat at his desk with head down, reading. He took off his glasses and pointed to Fen's preferred chair. "Did you eat lunch?"

Fen nodded.

"Want a cup of coffee?"

"I'm jacked up enough without another stimulant."

Chuck brushed aside the statement. "Relax. The way Tom and I have this planned, you'll stay in here listening until everyone's seated and Tom introduces you. He and two other highway patrol officers will set the tone for the meeting."

"No Texas Rangers?"

A shake of Chuck's head answered the question, but didn't give an explanation.

"Why not?" asked Fen.

"My understanding is that after they heard the details, they want to keep what happens here today as low key as possible." Chuck took a drink from a Diet Coke. "By the way, this is Tom's last week as a state trooper before he retires."

Fen chuckled. "It will take him another week to fill out all the paperwork."

Chuck's intercom came to life. "Danni Worth just pulled up," said Candy.

Chuck looked at his watch as he rose from his chair. "She's early."

"Was she surprised when you told her she'd need to come today?"

"Not when I told her she'd need to verify many of the things in today's newspaper."

"How are people around town reacting?"

Chuck responded as he headed to the door. "Between the rumors and Lou's previous articles, they're not surprised. Disgusted with Lori's performance, but not surprised." Chuck had his hand on the doorknob when he added, "Sit at my desk. The intercom from the conference room is on so you can hear your cue to come in."

The door closed with a firm click. It reminded Fen of the sound of a key turning in the lock of a cell door. He went to the other side of the desk and waited. It wasn't long before he heard Chuck take the lead in casual conversation with Danni. She sounded like she always did: friendly, confident, and sure of herself without being pushy.

The next people to arrive were Lori Newman and her fiancée, Jake Creech. After making sure nobody wanted a bottle of water, Chuck spoke loud enough for Fen to hear clearly. "Lieutenant, you're not in uniform today."

"I resigned," said Creech. "We moved the wedding up by two weeks, so I gave my notice."

Lori broke into the conversation with a crisp, "Mr. Forsythe, you should know that my father's attorney is busy suing that sorry excuse for a local newspaper. I have officers on the way to arrest the owner, editor, and that know-it-all reporter, Lou Cooper."

Creech spoke next. "You'll have to excuse her, Mr. Forsythe. It's been a distressing day for Lori and her father."

"I can imagine," said Chuck. "That's why the Department of Public Safety asked to use this conference room. State law enforcement takes defamation and overreach by the press seriously. Reporters have many protections under the law, but not carte blanche to ruin people's lives without reliable sources or evidence to back up their stories."

Lori leaned forward. "That's exactly what my father's attorney told me this morning."

Fen heard noises, but they sounded distant. Then Lori spoke again. "Daddy! Take those handcuffs off my father."

Tom Stevens's voice rang out. "He refused to come on his own, so he's being detained until I can investigate if he needs to be arrested or not."

Lori shouted, "You can't do that!"

"I can, and I'm warning you, Sheriff, don't press me on this."

Fen let out a soft whistle and then wondered if the intercom gave away his noise to those in the conference room. He held his breath until he heard Tom Stevens say, "Turn around and I'll get the cuffs off you, Mr. Newman."

The room went quiet except for the sound of handcuffs

rattling and chairs moving. Tom said, "Two more troopers will join us then I'll get started on my investigation."

"Not without my lawyer present," demanded Mr. Newman.

"You're not under arrest, but you are being detained while I investigate."

Chuck spoke up. "You don't have to say anything, Mr. Newman, and I think that's good free advice in this situation."

Lori chimed in, "Listen to Mr. Forsythe, Daddy."

Fen heard a voice in the hall that sounded like Candy, but he couldn't be sure. A door opened and closed. He moved to the door and cracked it open enough to take a peek. All he saw was the back of two state troopers, a male and female, as they entered the conference room.

Lori's voice rang out over the intercom. "You! Arrest her, Jake."

"I can't. I'm not on the force anymore."

"Well, I sure can."

Tom's deep voice boomed. "No one's getting arrested until I say so. If there's anyone who doesn't know her, this is Ms. Lou Cooper. She's going to explain why she believes everything she's written is accurate."

Fen ran his hand through his hair. "I wish I could see what's going on." He stared at the intercom and heard Tom say, "There's one more person who will join us. He's been feeding information to us from the very beginning. You can come in now."

Fen swallowed, walked down the hall, opened the door to the conference room, and stepped into a room full of unsmiling people.

Chapter Twenty Six

"What's he doing here?" demanded Lori.

Mr. Newman talked over her. "I'll not stay in the same room as the man who killed my daughter."

Jake Creech looked lost and confused.

Lori reached for her purse but didn't get far. All three uniformed state troopers had hands on pistols, ready to draw. Tom Stevens hollered, "Stop!"

He lowered his voice. "If anyone in this room has a weapon, raise both hands in the air."

People looked at each other but didn't move. Tom's next command blasted out, "Do it now!"

Lori raised hers first. Jake Creech hesitated until Tom moved to him and tapped with his finger on the table. "Put it right here, Jake."

The female trooper took the handbag from Lori and removed a small .9 mm as Jake pulled out a handgun from a shoulder holster.

"Anyone else?" asked Tom. "What about you, Danni?"

"I'm just a crime scene processor. I carry rubber gloves and paper booties in my purse."

"What about you, Ms. Cooper?"

"I fight with a pen." She held her jacket open and turned to the female officer. "Pat me down and check my purse if you think it's necessary."

The officer accepted the invitation and came up with nothing that resembled a firearm.

"They already searched me," said Mr. Newman.

Tom motioned for the male officer to take Jake's pistol from the table. Both troopers took out the clips, cleared the weapons, and placed the empty firearms on a table alongside a coffee maker. The male officer moved to stand in front of the door, while the female walked backward to a far corner.

"Why didn't you search Fen?" demanded Lori.

Fen took off his jacket, raised his hands and turned a slow circle. "I quit carrying a weapon when you took over as sheriff." He then moved to the far end of the table and sat near Candy, away from the clutch of people nearest the door. Lou went down the other side of the table and sat facing him.

Tom Stevens drew everyone's attention to the head of the table nearest the door when he said, "Now that we've made the room a safer place to conduct business, I'd like Ms. Cooper to review the highlights of her story in today's newspaper. So far, Sheriff Newman has ordered the arrest of the paper's owner, editor, and you. Tell me why I shouldn't allow her to take you to jail."

Lou stood with shoulders pinned back and a look of calm determination in her eyes. "I built my articles around seven separate facts or events. Each one points to Mr. Newman's likely involvement in various crimes. I'll take them in chronological order and tell you my source of information unless it's from a confidential informant. I assure you, everything I'm going to say is true."

Mr. Newman sputtered a laugh. "Everything she writes is a lie."

Lou lifted her chin and faced Mr. Newman. "I take no pleasure in writing about criminal activities, but a free press is essential to the health and wellbeing of society. There's something rotten in this town, in this county, and I only reported what I've discovered."

Tom Stevens adjusted his gun belt. "Now that you and Mr. Newman have discussed the benefits and drawbacks of a free press, let's move along. You mentioned things that form the basis of your articles. Summarize them."

Lou wasted no more time. "I monitor police traffic, so I was aware that Mr. Maguire discovered a body in the river that runs along his property. Like any reporter worth her salt, I went to investigate."

Lori interrupted. "She had no right to be there. It's private property, posted with 'No Trespassing' signs. Also, it was an active crime scene."

Tom looked at Fen with raised eyebrows.

"I gave Ms. Cooper permission to be there, and told her she needed to stay far enough away that she didn't interfere."

"And I complied," said Lou.

"No, you didn't," said Lori. "You stood so close you could hear every word."

Tom looked at Lori. "Don't forget, I was there. It was your crime scene. You could have made her move back."

Lori looked at her fiancée. "You should have told me."

Lou continued, "Out of courtesy, I put nothing in my original story about Sheriff Newman getting lost and stuck, which delayed her arrival."

A vein in Lori's neck bulged, and her face turned pink. Fen

didn't know if it was anger or embarrassment, but he headed off her response by stating, "Lou never crossed the police tape after they strung it along the river. Once Lori and Lieutenant Creech took over, they did an excellent job."

It wasn't the whole truth, but the words 'excellent job' seemed to mollify Lori a little. She unclenched her fists. But not for long.

Lou continued with her tale of the events. "According to records I received from the sheriff's office, Sergeant Tom Stevens sent a highway patrol officer to seal off the boat ramp; he believed that location might be the original crime scene. I noted in a subsequent article that land owned by Mr. Newman surrounds the boat ramp, except for the highway, the bridge, and the boat launch."

Lori waved her hand. "Don't you see where this is going? She intended to smear my father from the very beginning. She planted little seeds in the reader's minds by associating what we believe to be the murder site with land owned by my father."

Lou bristled. "I printed facts that I documented through courthouse records. Is it a crime in this county to print the truth?"

Silence.

Lou kept going. "This brings us to what they found at the boat ramp and in the river. Since some people have a hard time dealing with the truth, I'll ask Crime Scene Investigator Danni Worth to tell you what she found."

Danni looked at Tom, who gave her a nod. She stood. "We found no useful evidence on the property belonging to Mr. Maguire, other than the Justice of the Peace ruled the death a homicide and ordered an autopsy. His search of the body for injuries revealed a small hole at the base of the brain. He estimated a small caliber gun had caused the fatal injury. A subsequent autopsy proved his assumption correct."

"Tell us about finding the pistol," said Tom.

Danni nodded. "I recovered a pistol in the river at the boat launch in water I estimated to be three to four feet deep."

"Back to the autopsy," said Fen. "What other results were stated?"

Danni nodded. "The pathologist removed a .22 caliber round from the victim's brain. Forensic experts at the state crime lab matched it to the pistol I found in the river. Also, there were substantial amounts of barbiturates in Cletus Brumbaugh's system."

Lou interrupted, "As you can tell, we're not going in chronological order, but all the facts remain the same." She looked at Danni. "Since we're talking about the pistol that was recovered, what else can you tell us about it?"

"Sheriff Newman purchased the pistol used to kill Cletus Brumbaugh prior to her becoming sheriff."

Lori's next words came out fast and harsh. "And I gave it to my father, and someone stole it from him."

Lou quickly added, "Which was never reported to the police."

Mr. Newman spoke up. "It was in my truck this past summer because I killed a cotton mouth snake with it. I don't know when someone took it out of my truck."

Tom asked, "Why didn't you report it lost or stolen?"

"Lori gave it to me as a birthday present. I planned on replacing it with the same model, but hadn't done it yet."

A few seconds of silence followed until Tom said, "I'm not sure what else you want to add, but go ahead, Ms. Cooper."

"I found an interesting coincidence that I haven't put in print yet. Former sheriff's deputy Salinski received a tip that marijuana was being grown on property belonging to Mr.

Newman. The anonymous source told Salinski where to patrol late at night. He was involved in a chase which resulted in an accident and life-threatening injuries. The reported source of the drugs was on Newman land."

"Jake investigated that incident," said Lori. "Salinski lost control, and this is the first I've heard about there being drugs."

Fen looked at Lori. "Did you ask Ski?"

Jake answered for her. "I tried. He couldn't speak when I last saw him."

"When was that?" asked Lou.

Lori bristled. "None of your business."

Tom took over again. "Let's get back to Ms. Cooper's list. We can circle back to Officer Salinski if we need to."

"Next," said Lou, "the victim, Cletus Brumbaugh. I learned from reliable sources that Clete lived rent free in a trailer on land owned by Mr. Newman."

The aging multi-millionaire sat up straight. "He promised to fix the place up. He built a nice back porch and kept the yard looking good for a while, but over time he let it go to ruin. I meant to run him off, but his niece moved in at the end of summer and I didn't have the heart."

Lou continued where she left off. "My sources told me that the real reason Mr. Newman allowed Clete to live in the trailer is because it would cost too much to have the trailer moved. He has quite the reputation for thrift."

No one contradicted her, so Lou moved on. "Clete's niece, Bailey Madison, lived in the trailer by herself after his murder. She showed her talent as an artist at the Fall Festival, working alongside Mr. Maguire. While they were away at a Halloween Carnival, an arsonist set fire to Mr. Newman's trailer. I reported that Mr. Maguire and Ms. Madison returned to the trailer sooner than expected and found the fire raging. Ms. Madison received serious injuries trying to recover possessions and Mr. Maguire required hospitalization overnight."

"I didn't set that fire," said Mr. Newman in a firm voice.

"I published nothing saying you did," said Lou.

Lori's chin quivered, and she pointed with a shaking hand. "You didn't have to. By that time, everyone believed my father was a killer. You wanted people to think he's also an arsonist. Your stories are like the blows from an ax. One won't kill a tree, but you keep swinging, taking out chunks of his good name. You're trying to ruin him, and I want to know why."

Lou tented her hands on hips. "It's called collecting facts that lead to truth. I know it's a foreign concept these days, but I back up my stories with quotes and facts. There's a link between every crime we've discussed and your father. Both you and your father admit to him receiving the pistol as a gift. There's no disputing the forensic evidence that his weapon was used to kill Clete Brumbaugh. What do you expect from a person who writes for a newspaper?"

Tom looked at Chuck. "Off the record, I'd like a legal opinion on what you've heard so far. Is there enough evidence to arrest Mr. Newman?"

Lori hung her head while Jake Creech looked on with rapt attention to what the attorney would say.

Chuck hesitated, then said, "There's more than enough for an arrest on the murder charge. I'd hold off on the arson. The D.A. can always add that later. Remember, I'm not talking about a conviction. Juries can do strange things, and I have a feeling there will be a lot more evidence uncovered once you make an arrest."

Fen wiggled in his chair and raised his hand. "Tom, I hate to do this, but I had seconds of iced tea at lunch. I have to take a quick break."

"Oh, good grief," said Lou. "Your timing stinks."

"Go ahead, Fen. I need to make a phone call." Tom looked at Lou. "You can also leave, Ms. Cooper. Thank you for your input in this matter."

"No way. I've earned a place at this table and I'm staying."

Fen shifted his weight from one foot to the other and back again. "Come on, Lou. You don't want to leave here wearing handcuffs."

Lou glared at him. "That will only make the story better."

"Come on." He gave her a conspiratorial wink. "We're wasting time that I don't have." He shifted his weight faster.

Lou gave her head a firm shake. He leaned down and whispered. "I know a way you can listen and not get arrested."

She gave him a furtive stare and whispered, "Are you lying?"

He headed for the door. "Suit yourself. I'll be looking for your mug shot in your next article."

He heard a chair move behind him. He opened the door, but didn't wait for Lou to walk out before him. She closed the door. His full bladder dance came to an abrupt end. In a low voice, he said, "Follow me to Chuck's office. You and I are going to have a quick conversation. I'll talk and you listen for a change."

"You don't need a pit stop?"

"Of course not." He guided her by the elbow until they entered Chuck's office and he shut the door behind them.

Chapter Twenty-Seven

Fen took three steps into Chuck's office and turned to face Lou. The problem was his lower leg didn't keep up with everything above the knee. Pain shot through him and he found himself with his arms wrapped around her, using her as a pole to hang onto.

"Are you all right?"

He looked into wide eyes with milk-chocolate irises. "Sorry. Help me to the couch."

"Is it bad this time?" asked Lou after they untangled and he had only one arm around her shoulder.

He leaned heavily on her and took a tentative step, testing his weight. "I'll let you know when I try to bend it. If I scream like a little girl, I'll be out of commission for a while." After a few more stiff-leg steps he half sat, half fell, on the couch.

Lou pushed the coffee table close to his leg and gently lifted it as he did all he could to help her elevate it. The expression of concern on her face waned. "Has anyone ever talked to you about lousy timing?"

He forced a grin. "You told me my timing stinks a few minutes ago."

This earned a short-lived grin. She moved around the coffee table and sat facing him, with her hip almost touching his throbbing knee. "Start talking, Fen, and it better be good. I'll not miss out on this story."

"You don't have to if you promise you'll do one little thing."

Her head tilted, and distrust replaced the compassion in her voice. "I won't tell a lie."

"What about omit the whole truth a little?"

"You're not making sense. Is it because of the pain?"

He shook his head. "I want you to tell the story of what's about to happen in the conference room. The facts of what you'll hear are all true. The only thing that might be a little off is who discovered what will lead up to the arrests."

"Arrests?"

He nodded. "Plural."

"I'm listening."

Fen rubbed his knee and gave it the first tentative bend. "That's good," he said. "No shooting pain." He leaned back. "Like I was saying, arrests are going to take place, at least two and possibly three. You'll need to have the camera on your phone ready."

Lou let out a huff. "There's plenty of bait on the hook already. Tell me in plain words how much you want me to shade the truth and I'll tell you yes or no."

Fen leaned forward and looked her dead in her right eye. "I want Tom Stevens to get full credit for solving this case. I discovered two critical pieces of information that will exonerate Nathaniel Newman from all guilt." He paused. "He's still guilty of hating me and slander, but those aren't important."

Lou leaned away from his stare. "I've been a reporter long enough to have known a couple of cops like you. Only two because they seem to be a dying breed. You don't care who gets the credit for doing the digging and finding things buried so deep others can't see or even smell them."

She turned to look away and spoke in a tone that sounded like defeat. "This means you'll take months of my work and put a match to it."

Fen paired the volume of his words to hers. "You reported the truth as you saw it."

"Don't you mean you had people spoon-feed it to me?" She looked back at him. "Oh well, I was looking for a job when I found this one."

"It might not come to that. You'll have the exclusive on this one and most everyone in the county will be happy to have Tom as the new sheriff. They'll soon forget the stories that pointed to Mr. Newman's guilt. Don't forget, you never actually accused him of anything."

She tucked her hair behind her ear. "All right, Mr. Maguire, you have a deal. I won't mention that you're a private investigator or that it was you who cracked the case. I'll also be careful to give Tom Stevens credit for solving it, with one caveat. If anyone in that room says anything about your involvement, I'll print it."

Fen smiled. "Mention my name a time or two, but spin the stories to point to Tom." He bent his knee and eased his right foot to the floor. "So far, so good, only moderate pain. Give me a hand up."

They almost made it to the door when it opened in front of them. Chuck saw Fen with his arm over Lou's shoulder and scowled. "This is a lousy time for that knee to go out on you."

Fen chuckled. "That's the third time someone's criticized me for bad timing. I'll work on it."

Lou passed him off to Chuck and Fen walked without too much pain as long as he leaned on his attorney.

Candy saw them coming down the hallway and shook her head. "I'll get the ice packs. Chuck, get a chair and stick that peg-leg of his in it."

All eyes shifted to stare at Fen and Chuck as they entered the room. No one paid attention to Lou as she retrieved her phone from her purse.

After Candy returned with ice packs and nestled them on Fen's knee, she nodded to Tom Stevens.

Tom cleared his throat. "In case there's still someone here who believes that there's not enough evidence for me to arrest Mr. Newman, let me add one more thing on the pile." He looked at Danni. "Ms. Worth. Would you tell us about the gas can that's gone missing?"

Danni stood, opened a folder, and took out an enlarged photo of a gas can. "I took this the day after the fire at the trailer. As you can see, what remains of the trailer is in the background. This can contained gasoline used to start and speed up the fire. It's a little hard to make out, but written on the can is NEWMAN in a black marker."

Lori hung her head, but Mr. Newman wasn't going down without a fight. "Someone must have stolen it out of the back of my truck."

Lou spoke up. "First the pistol and now a gas can?"

Tom raised his hands to quieten Lou. He faced Danni again. "Did you turn the gas can over to the sheriff's department?"

"Yes. To the sheriff."

"Is that true, Lori?"

She nodded. "Danni gave it to me and I handed it to Lieutenant Creech."

"Then where is it?"

"It should be in the property room," said Creech.

"It's in my office closet," said Lori.

Tom pursed his lips and shook his head, showing displeasure. "I'll need to get that from you today before it gets lost."

Tom stood straight. "We're almost finished, but there are a couple more things to go over. I'd like to call on Fen Maguire to tell us what he found at the burned-out trailer."

"Pardon me if I don't get up." Fen looked around the room as eyes locked on him. "I believe everyone knows Sam, my ranch foreman. Several days after the fire, he drove me to the remains of the trailer so we could look for anything that belonged to Bailey and to pick up her bicycle. Before Mr. Newman came along and accused me of trespassing, I noticed something on the property that wasn't consumed in the fire. It was an outhouse, tucked away in the backyard, under a canopy of trees. Something about it didn't look right, so Sam and I went to inspect it. We noticed that the construction was fairly new, but made to look old. Also, the dimensions didn't fit those of any outhouse I'd ever seen. I called Tom about it."

Jake Creech broke his silence. "You should have called the sheriff's office."

Fen nodded in agreement. "I would have, but my relationship with some people there isn't what you'd call congenial."

Tom took over and all eyes shifted back to the highway patrol sergeant. "What myself and other state troopers found was a large quantity of marijuana in black garbage bags." He paused. "We also found a journal of sorts. Some sort of code. I couldn't crack it, so I sent it on to DPS headquarters in Austin."

"Have you broken it yet?" asked Danni.

"Before I answer that, I want to show you a video that was taken by someone who happened upon the fire."

Fen held up his hand. "That would be me and Bailey. She was driving because this trick leg of mine doesn't like Halloween carnivals near as much as Harvest Festivals. I had Sam install cameras on all our vehicles and Bailey turned them on when she saw flames and smoke in the distance. This is the video she captured."

Tom had the television remote in his hand and in a matter of seconds, everyone in the room was staring at a fifty-inch television mounted on the wall. It took a few minutes as Fen's truck drew ever-closer to smoke and flames. As they flew past the Friendly Baptist Church, they passed a black Ford pickup traveling in the opposite direction. Because of the speed of the two vehicles, it was nothing but a blur.

The recording kept playing as Fen narrated. "We're turning into the driveway. As you can see, Bailey parked too near the fire, immediately got out, and went around the building. And there I am, walking like a one-leg pirate, trying to catch up with her. She went to the back porch and tried to get in. That's where she burned her hand."

Everyone remained quiet, and only the sounds of the inferno filled the room. Long minutes later, the paint on the hood of the truck bubbled, and the truck backed out of the driveway, stopped on the road, and sped toward town. The only other thing of interest was the passing of the responding fire truck and Fen's arrival at the hospital.

Tom paused the television when Fen passed in front of his truck in a wheelchair. "I had the wizards in Austin put together a few clips from the recording you just saw, as well as other shots from other cameras Fen had mounted on his truck."

Lou turned to Fen and gave a nod of approval. He wondered if she would want Sam to mount cameras on her Camry.

The first clip was in slow motion. It showed the trailer's driveway as Bailey pulled in. Tom asked, "Does anyone see what's missing?"

Several seconds passed before Lou said, "There's no gas can."

"You're very observant, Ms. Cooper," said Tom as he scanned everyone in the room. "Hang on to that bit of information. It will become important later on."

With the push of a button, the scene on the television screen changed to a slowed down version of Fen and Bailey approaching the small country church. "Look closely," said Tom. "You can see a vehicle turn off the county road that runs in front of the trailer." He allowed the tape to run. "The black truck turns and is now coming toward Mr. Maguire's truck. I'll take it frame by frame right before the vehicles pass each other."

The shots showed blurred images of the driver and the license plate

"I can't make it out," said Danni.

"Me either," said Jake Creech. "The high-beam headlights from the other truck blinded the camera, just like they do the driver. No plates. No description of the driver."

"Let's look at another view," said Tom. "This is from the camera in Fen's truck that gives us a rear shot. Again, this will be in slow motion."

Without the oncoming headlights, the rear license plate shone clear and bright. Tom turned to the former lieutenant. "Mr. Creech, that's your truck, and it's you driving it." The image on the screen changed to a blown-up image of Jake looking in the large side mirror, his face clearly illuminated. "Can you explain why you left the scene of a fire without reporting it?"

Jake clamped his lips shut, but Sheriff Lori didn't follow his example. "What are you saying? Are you implying Jake burned down that trailer?"

Tom rested his forearm on the butt of his pistol. "I'm not only implying it, I'm arresting him for arson. I'm sure other charges will follow."

"You can't do that to me. This is some sort of conspiracy you cooked up with Fen."

Tom ignored the comment and motioned to the male patrolman. "Cuff him, get him out of here, read him his rights, and hand Mr. Creech over to the officers in the parking lot."

"Where are you taking him?" demanded Lori.

"Over the river and into the next county. It's standard procedure in cases like this."

Lou made no attempt to be discreet as she snapped a half-dozen photos.

Fen noticed the look of relief on Mr. Newman's face and wondered if he was happy to hold on to his four thousand acres of prime land, or if it was the realization the law was looking at someone besides him. Perhaps it was the realization he'd not have another son-in-law he'd end up hating.

"I'm going with him," said Lori.

Tom gave her a look that reminded Fen of the way a father stares at a teen caught drinking and driving. "Sit down, Lori. I don't want to detain you, but I will if necessary."

Tom looked around the room. "One more thing to clear up and we'll be through. Mr. Maguire told you about the outhouse that survived the fire and I told you we discovered a large amount of marijuana. Our investigation revealed this came from a crop grown on the adjacent land, also owned by Mr. Newman."

"I wouldn't know a marijuana plant from a petunia," bellowed Mr. Newman.

"I believe you," said Tom. He looked at Danni. "If you're wondering why we didn't call you in to do the crime scene investigation, it's because we found your log."

"What log?"

"The one Clete kept of all his drug sales, and the cut you and Jake took from him. You two must have thought he kept the log in the trailer. That's why you conspired with Creech to burn the evidence. You weren't counting on Clete building an outhouse and storing his products and records there."

Danni wasn't having any of it. "I was at the Halloween Carnival when the fire trucks left. How many witnesses do you want me to present?"

"None. Remember the gas can? It wasn't in the driveway when Fen left the fire to go to the hospital. None of the first responders remembered seeing it until after you arrived on the scene the next morning."

"If that's all the evidence you have, you have a lousy case."

"That's not all," said Tom. "While Fen and Lou took a break, I made a phone call. State troopers with warrants conducted searches of your home and Jake Creech's. Not only did they find a ledger very similar to the one we discovered in the outhouse, they also found the book on crime scene photography you used to make your code. It's an old trick to find a couple copies of an out-of-print book and use it to make a code. Page number, paragraph, and word count identify words. If you have an obscure book or two, it's almost impossible to break the code. It was your bad luck, Danni, that you chose a book Fen had on his bookshelf."

Danni's face fell, but Tom kept talking. "We also found the holster that goes with the pistol you fished out of the river. It didn't go unnoticed that you knew where to look in the river. It was a pretty easy find."

Lou was on her feet with her phone clicking photos while handcuffs went on Danni.

Tom had one final thing to say. "Texas Rangers are waiting for Jake across the county line. They can be very persuasive in questioning felony suspects."

Chapter Twenty-Eight

Fen and Lou sat on the couch in Chuck's office as all three waited for Candy to arrive with a pen and notepad. Chuck wasn't one to allow a conversation to lag so he said, "Hard to believe it's already been a week since Tom arrested Danni Worth and Jake Creech." He lifted his coffee mug to Lou and issued what looked to be a toast. "Great job on the stories. I particularly liked the banner headline: *State Cop Cleans County.*"

"I appreciate the way you gave Tom credit," said Fen.

"Readers love a hero," replied Lou. "Even if he had someone behind the curtain pulling the levers." She took a quick breath. "By the way, Great Oz, how's the knee?"

"Good. Like always, all I have to do is ice it a couple of days, don't turn too quickly, and everything goes back in place."

Candy stepped through the doorway in time to hear his explanation. "If you had a knee replacement, you wouldn't have to worry about ice and rest."

"You know I can't stand hospitals. They make me break out in poverty."

Candy spoke as she took her seat alongside Chuck. Both faced Fen and Lou. "You must have received Bailey's hospital bill."

"Three weeks in the hospital with very specialized surgeries doesn't come cheap. Bailey and I will need to sell a lot of paintings."

"We might be able to help a bit," said Chuck.

Candy interrupted him before he could expound. "Tell me, Fen, did you enjoy being a private investigator?"

His answer came back quickly. "I've thought about it this past week, and the answer is yes. It surprised me how much I enjoyed it. Of course, this was an unusual case. I particularly liked it when I fooled Danni and Creech into thinking I wasn't doing anything."

Lou turned to him. "Off the record. When did you first suspect Danni killed Clete?"

"I thought something smelled fishy when she found the pistol with such ease. There was a big, wide river to throw that gun in. Why was it pitched in shallow water by the boat ramp?"

Fen took a sip of coffee. "My suspicion of her grew when she came to see me at my home after she found the gun. The body being found on my land was bad luck for her. She knew me well enough to suspect I'd investigate."

"Ah," said Lou. "How did you convince her you weren't?"

"I'm not sure I did for quite a while. I had to stick to my story. Over time, I lulled her into a sense of safety, so she continued her plan to use Jake Creech to get to Lori, and blame Mr. Newman for the murder. Her attempt to get information from me backfired when she admitted she knew Creech when they worked in the next county over. I did some checking and found out they knew each other much better than Danni led me to believe."

"But Creech was going to marry Lori Newman," said Lou.

Fen smiled. "Getting married and staying married are two different things. Danni told me she liked to play the long game. She could wait until Mr. Newman went to prison for something she and Jake cooked up. He'd likely turn over control of his estate to Lori. The key to their plan was for Jake to marry Lori. After that, Jake would run the sheriff's office from behind a curtain and tell Lori what to do with Daddy's land."

Chuck chimed in. "There's no telling what they would have done if that happened."

Fen finished the thought. "Up to, and including, making sure Lori had a tragic accident. After all, who better to plan and execute a murder than a crime scene investigator?"

Lou let out a low whistle. "That would put Jake in line to control the estate: land, oil, cattle, everything."

"Exactly," said Fen. "The perfect setup for Danni and Creech. They'd control much of the law enforcement in the county and have all the money they needed to stay in power."

Fen took a swig of coffee. "What's the latest on Danni and Creech? Have they turned on each other yet?"

Chuck gave a sly smile. "Once the DA offered Creech eighteen years for the arson charge and dropped the murder, Creech found his memory and his voice. Danni did the shooting. The fact they found the holster in her possession sealed the deal."

In an abrupt change of conversation, Chuck asked, "Fen, would you like to keep doing what you did in cleaning up this county?"

Fen shrugged. "I already told you I enjoyed it, but there won't be much left to clean up after Tom is sheriff."

"Which won't be long," said Candy. "Lori turned in her resignation, and Tom's being named interim sheriff until they hold a special election."

"How would you know that?" asked Fen.

"That's not important right now," said Candy. "What's important is you telling us if you'd like to continue doing special assignments around the state and possibly around the country."

"As a private detective?"

Candy nodded.

"Do I have to carry a gun?"

She shook her head. "Not if you don't want to."

"What kind of cases?"

"Serious ones."

"Who's behind this offer?"

"Good people who believe in justice and playing by the rules."

Fen rubbed his chin. "Can you be more specific?"

"Just like you did in this case, we like to stay out of sight." Candy smiled. "There's not too many of us, but enough to make a difference."

Fen turned to look at Lou. "You wouldn't be here if you weren't part of this cloak and dagger operation."

Lou chuckled. "Nice deduction, detective. I'm what you might call a useful distraction. While I stirred up a stink in the press, you found out who was plotting a hostile takeover of the county."

Candy took over again. "If Mr. Newman hadn't bought enough votes to elect Lori in the last election, Lou wouldn't be here. We thought reporting the truth would be enough to straighten things out, but everything escalated when Clete floated down the Brazos. We were planning on bringing in another PI until you contacted Chuck and let us know you were looking into the murder."

Fen shifted in his seat. "I'm intrigued, but the practical side of me is wondering how much of a time commitment I'm looking at. Also, if I'm off investigating murders and who knows what else, how am I supposed to make a living?"

"That's simple," said Candy. "Continue to paint and do fairs and exhibits. It's a great cover story for you to travel. Don't act surprised if you get commissions out of the blue."

A memory pushed its way to the top of Fen's mind. "That explains what Judge Rawlings was doing at the Harvest Festival. He could have called me if he wanted another landscape."

Lou added, "A publisher contacted me out of the blue. I now have a two-book deal that will supplement my income nicely."

Fen shook his head in wonder. "Whoever it is better have some deep pockets to pay Bailey's medical bills."

"You can throw those away," said Chuck. "There was an error in billing. Bailey qualified as indigent."

Fen used his coffee as a way of delaying a response. He set it on the table and looked into three expectant faces. "I'll do one more case and see how it suits me."

Candy hadn't written a word on her notepad, but she flipped the cover shut. "Chuck will call you."

Fen let out a moan. "Hold on. There's something I forgot. If I'm doing fairs, Bailey will want to go with me. She's intent on making a living painting."

Candy stood. "Once she's healed, take her with you. It's the perfect story. A traveling artist and his star pupil doing shows and looking for interesting things to paint. She helped you solve this case. Perhaps she can be of use in the next one."

Chuck went into a closet and returned to his desk with a green file folder. He looked first at Fen, then Lou. "You two might want to get prepared to travel. There's trouble brewing in East Texas along the Angelina River."

From The Author

Thank you for reading *Murder On The Brazos.* I hope you enjoyed this first Fen Maguire Mystery. If you loved it, please consider leaving a review at your favorite retailer, Bookbub or Goodreads. Your reviews help other readers discover their next great mystery!

If you would like to get in on the fun that surrounds the writing of my books, join my mystery-loving reader community. You'll be among the first to know about new releases, discounts and recommendations. After you sign up you'll receive the first perk of being a Mystery Insider, the prequel to the Fen Maguire Mysteries!

Happy Reading!
Bruce

You may scan below to sign up or go to
brucehammack.com/the-fen-maguire-mysteries-prequel/.

Murder On The Angelina

There's more to this game than dodging paintballs… a killer is on the loose.

When private investigator Fen Maguire is called upon to investigate an extortion ring putting the squeeze on loggers in East Texas, the clues lead him to the local championship paintball team. The tight-lipped community of loggers and team supporters block his inquiries at every turn. When the team's leader is killed mid match, Fen must break through the wall of resistance or a killer will get away with murder.

Scan the image below to get your copy or go to brucehammack.com/books/murder-on-the-angelina/.

About The Author

Drawing from his extensive background in criminal justice, Bruce Hammack writes contemporary, clean read detective and crime mysteries. He is the author of the Smiley and McBlythe Mysteries, the Fen Maguire Mysteries and the Star of Justice series. Having lived in eighteen cities around the world, he now lives in the Texas hill country with his wife of thirty-plus years.

Be sure to follow Bruce on Bookbub and Goodreads for the latest new release info and recommendations. Learn more at brucehammack.com.

Made in the USA
Las Vegas, NV
28 February 2025

18834139R00132